Paul F

Red Town
White Town

Clayton Books
Loris, South Carolina

Cover art: Herd of Deer in a Maple Grove

Artist unknown - Circa 951 A.D.

This is a work of fiction. Although some characters like John Wright, Thomas Nairne, Charles Craven, Francis Le Jau, and George Chicken were all public figures and did live in the Carolinas, at the time of the Tuscarora and Yamasee conflicts, all of the dialogue here is of my own invention, and any similarities to above said persons own written accounts, or the written accounts of others is completely coincidental.

"Traders make a living off a getting slaves - period - end of story. Cause ain't nothing else so valuable or so easily portable as a live human being. So sometimes they stir em up - even if it ain't Big Spring time, the normal season for fighting. Stir em up and have em go knock heads - like that Bellamy feller did with them Waterees in the Wintertime too. He got the Cherokee to rub em out just so's he could line his own pockets.

-- John Wright - Carolina Indian Agent, 1711

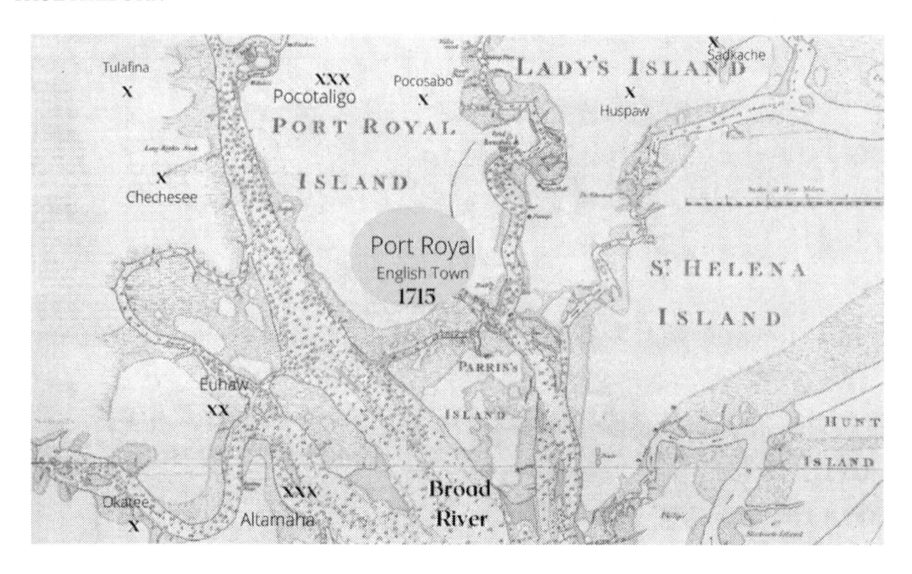

The Ten Towns of the Yamasee surrounding Port Royal - 1715

Red Towns (War)	White Towns (Peace)
Pocotaligo	Euhaw
Altamaha	Tulafina
Huspaw	Okatee
Pocosabo	Tomotly
	Chechesee
	Sadkache

X - 100 people

XXX - 300 people

CHAPTER 1

THE RECONNAISSANCE - JANUARY 1713

The mockingbird flies over and looks down at 22 canoes paddling upriver fast with the rising tide. It is midwinter and near noon, bright and sunny. Bald cypress conifers lie thick along the banks, blocking out the rest of the trees. The trunks are as wide as a man is tall, with roots like giant crab legs stretching out into the waters. They all have a tilt to them, leaning in towards the river; a wall of grey with splashes of green spreading out behind. The limbs are bare as a spiders web, like roots reaching up to the sky. The mockingbird sees plenty of good purchases, but he is watching the men intently now and circles, gliding past the cypress stand again - and then back to the boats.

The men all row in unison. Two to a canoe, except for one man - the Captain - who sits very still in the middle of the third canoe, which is bit longer than the rest. They paddle fast, close to 7 knots, yet 14 knots less than the mockingbird flies though, so he circles them again and again. On the last turn he sees some smoke away off and decides to go check that out too. He lands in a giant cypress, a big bald one, just up the river, where he can see clearly for miles all around.

The water below is moving fast and glittering. Mockingbird looks again at the boats and sees the waves of their wakes refracting, glinting from the sunlight and the motion of the paddles.

They are a war group of Euhaw and Catawba Indians closing in on a Tuscarora band attacking a small Swiss settlement - a cow farm on a creek off the White Oak river - coastal North Carolina. The Tuscarora are whooping it up and taking their potshots - getting ready for the charge.

The Euhaw and Catawba are led by Captain George Chicken, and Coronet David Kilbernie, of the Broad River militia. The men with Chicken are 44 total - 3 White men, 41 Tribesmen - all armed with muskets. David carries a pistol and an older Scottish Claymore sword, two handed - in a scabbard strapped onto his back.

The Indians all have tomahawks and carry at least one knife, and some are carrying pistols too. All are wearing buckskins, with a wide variety of light lattice chest armor - mostly bamboo.

Matt, a tall Euhaw fighter who is fluent in English and Muscogee, and also the sole black man in the troop, reports first on the scouting.

"It's a long house with a log fence around it - like a cowpen filled in with dirt and rocks some. Best they could do I reckon - got six guns pointed out."

Matt snorts and shakes his head. "They's a little branch running out past the back side of it - and a big field on this side coming up - with a grove of pecan trees right before you get to that clearing." He shakes his head again and looks straight at Chicken.

"Ain't no lookouts at them trees, Cap'n, nor back of that branch, neither. They ain't got no lookouts, period." Matt smiles then says, "If we come up on 'em low and slow we can range a volley easy - two sides."

"How many fighters?", the Captain asks.

"I counted 25 head, all with muskets - look like new ones too. English made."

"Ever one?" Chicken is disgusted, unbelieving.

Matt is nodding, "Yep."

"Damn! Where in the hell did they get them guns from, Matt? -- They's supposed to be a ban on trade here." Chicken scowls and spits on the ground.

"Supposed to be is right. You will see." Matt's nodding and then adds.

"They got the blood up too, Cap'n. Won't be long now, I expect."

Chicken turns to David and Jeff and says, "What about it, Jeff? Draw me a picture, eh?"

Jeff shakes his head and says, "No. Let him say and draw." He looks to David, who picks up a stick and scribbles a quick sketch in the dirt of the layout, and pointing with the stick starts his report.

"Well... it's like Matt said. Here's the fence, and there's the wee crick there." David points. "And yeah, we can cross on that crick there and get a decent shot, maybe 50, 60 yards out - plenty a cover on both sides too. And they got no scouts posted anywhere, Cap'n - none that I saw. The whole of the perimeter is unwatched." He waves a circle around the drawing with the stick.

"Them folks ain't shooting back none. Out a balls I reckon." Matt says.

David nods, both of them looking at the captain. Chicken mulls it a bit and then grins. "Well... them folks is Swiss, eh? And mighty poor Swiss too, or they wouldn't be here now, would they? So it may be they's just being stingy with their lead, eh? Like a Scot - lookin to surprise yer!" He laughs and turns to David.

"Coronet, you and your Euhaw troop will move on up to this grove here," Chicken says, pointing to the drawing in the dirt. "I'll take the Catawba on around back of the creek there. You take your time now. Quiet's the word, eh? You get there and ... then... just wait." The captain grins big. "Just wait til them bucks make their run, by God! Let them run into a three way crossfire, eh? God's heart lads, we might can just take the whole bloody bunch!"

"I can show you best way back round to that branch, cap'n." Matt says.

"No, Johnboy can do that. You go on with Davey here. Keep an eye out for him now. You know this business here better than any." Chicken nods and points back to the dirt.

"You ease on up to that grove there - and then y'all just keep still, hear me? Ain't none o y'all shoots until you hear us give em a volley first, eh? That'll be your signal. Then y'all fire em up quick like, and come in a running."

"And don't nobody here - nobody - prime your bloody trigger pans til you bloody well get there - into position, eh! We shall have no accidental discharges. Not this close. Tell em." All the time Jeff is giving translations to the Catawba.

"25 fighters, so they's probably what, Matt? 40 women and chillerns close by?" Matt nods, as do the fighters around him. "So we got to keep some alive now, for questioning. Tell em, tell em any man what gives up the camp and takes us to it... He gets to live, him and his kin. Guaranteed. The Government's parole. And I'll cover the bounty on that scalp too. Double it!"

The men stir and murmur some as this last bit gets translated. David asks, "Is that what the Governor said, Cap'n?"

"No, but I aim to do it anyhow. Make em believe it, lads." He looks down to the drawing again and then back up and barks out, "Go on now! Knock some heads and take some scalps."

The Euhaw and Catawba leave off in two directions. Matt is walking next to David and asks, "What is parole?"

"Parole means they get to go free, long as they don't go to war against us again."

"Who all is us?"

CHAPTER 2

THE DOUBLE MASSACRE AT SYDNEY CREEK

The Tuscarora charge the Swiss before either war group gets to the flanks. Chicken arrives too late to see any of it, and David's group only sees the end. Since his orders are to wait until Chicken is in position and fires first, David tries to get the Euhaw to hold up.

"Wait, Wait," David yelps quiet-like, spins around and watches as the whole troop sprints away. Then he takes off too. He catches up with Jeff and the older fighters but is still about 10 yards behind the rest. Matt is in the lead and drifts to a high spot on the fence, brings his musket down and fires, as 14 more warriors do the same right and left beside him in a long, ragged volley. Then they vault the fence one or two handed, swinging tomahawks, and fast engaged in hand to hand fighting. David slows and veers to the right, at a lower spot - stops at the fence and shoots one Tuscarora with his musket. Then he sees Matt tomahawk another man in the head close by, taking him down. David takes his pistol out and shoots a fighter rushing up behind Matt - then glances left to see Jeff toss down his musket, vault the fence two handed and roll up tomahawking into another man.

David then drops his pistol and vaults over the fence two handed, reaches back, draws his sword and kills three more Tuscarora in a skipping frenzy that takes about three seconds, or three strokes of that big sword. The tomahawks hit so hard in the background that they make a light concussive retort - a hundred pops or more.

It is all settled inside of 30 seconds, including the run. -- The last shot is made by the oldest Euhaw fighter. He stays at the fence and shoots one man, just as he jumps up from the ground behind David, tomahawk raised. He's hit in the shoulder, spins and falls. David turns and sees all the bodies surrounding him - 16 Swiss dead, including women and children - 25 Tuscarora fighters down, dead or wounded, soon to be dead. The blood is everywhere, covering the ground, and splattered all over their buckskins and faces. It is a massacre twice done. Some Euhaw have cuts and bruises, but they are all still standing. The fighter at David's feet is stretching his arm again for a tomahawk. David stomps on his back, slaps the tomahawk away with the point of the blade and hollers back.

"Jeff! Ask this'n here where's that camp! Ask im."

CHAPTER 3

A NIGHT OF TORTURE

None of the Tuscarora talk. Except to make threats. Some sing songs. The threat makers all say, "No habla Ingles!" and taunt Jeff, the weary translator.

Jeff is disgusted, "They no say - no say! Light them! Let them show brave. This bunch no say. Light them up I say!"

The torturing lasts well into the night and is as hard a thing as David has ever witnessed ,as seven warriors are tied up to trees, scalped alive and stabbed with large splinters of fat lighter pine into their arms and legs; and then set on fire.

David is 19 years old, less than a year in the colony, and has never seen a man killed before today, except at a hanging.

CHAPTER 4

THE RAID ON THE WHITTOCK VILLAGE

Matt, Johnboy, David and Jeff scout the small Tuscarora town on the White Oak River. When they return Chicken asks Matt about the camp.

"They's about 40 of em Cap'n - mostly younguns. Got four old men with muskets holding some captures - two womens and three littlens - white folk. Them muskets is English too - same as what we just took."

Chicken nods his head and says, "Four guns then, that's it?"

Matt says, "Yep. Some of they womenfolk been known to keep bows though." Matt frowns.

"Draw me a picture, Davey." Chicken hands David a stick. He takes it and furrows out several long parallel lines.

"Well, they's about 100 yards or so off the river there. And it ain't a camp, but houses here and there, all spread out - and a big, big corn field what goes on for a half mile or so. The houses all run along next to that field, more or less."

"But right now they's all gathered at the lodge house here." David is drawing and pointing while he talks. "They got something big cooking. That's the smoke we saw. The captives are right at the lodge there, all tied up on one post - a sad looking bunch."

"No doubt." Chicken looks up. "Well lads, It looks like fortune has smiled upon us once again. Once again rounding them up all in one spot, nice and neat, eh? -- What would you suggest we do now then, Coronet? Another flanking maneuver, perhaps? But minus the volley?"

David looks down, and shaking his head answers, "Well ... I hope we can help them poor souls back there. Then... I don't know what. I signed up for this, I know. But I ain't... I just ... I ain't got no recommendation here, Captain."

Chicken has his eyes locked hard on David, with a matching grimace.

"Alright then. Once we make the charge you will range this perimeter, and keep a sharp eye outwards for more hostiles. Got that Coronet? Scout the perimeter, eh? Watch our backs while the rest of us here tend to business. Think ye can handle that?" David nods back.

In the ensuing "battle" the Euhaw attack one side with the Catawba on the other. They don't shoot first, but just run in and start knocking people down - rather gentle like compared to the ferocity of the day before. -- A lot of folks are running away, but one of the women takes up a bow and hits a Euhaw fighter in the guts with an arrow, and immediately after that Matt shoots her with his musket. Another woman with a bow is shot down before she can take good aim and misses, her arrow skewing up and away.

One old man is shot and killed, reaching for his gun, and one manages to shoot first but misses bad, then gets tomahawked hard by a big Catawba fighter - killed. The other two old men are knocked down easy by Jeff and Johnboy before they can get to their guns - both caught. Matt and the rest chase off after the runners and most of them are soon caught too; knocked or pushed down from behind while trying to run away. Then they get tied up in ropes, mostly, some easy, some with trouble.

Matt pushes one little girl down from behind while running after her, and she hits the ground so hard she bounces back up into his arms. Captain Chicken, Jeff, Johnboy, and the big

Catawba free the white captives - 2 women and 3 children.

So again in about 30 seconds time - 2 women and 2 old men killed. The captures taken number 2 old men, soon to be scalped - 14 women, and 24 children, later to be sold as slaves. Maybe some get away.

The mockingbirds are alarmed at all the commotion and make their warning calls as they circle around - higher and higher up - away from it all.

CHAPTER 5

DAVID TAKES A STAND

David shows up just before dusk with a pistol in hand and a sword at his hip. It's early still and the old men have not been hooked up to the poles yet. They just sit there. The Catawba and Euhaw are dealing with the spoils, not much besides the guns. The real value is in the captives themselves.

David has the pistol in his right hand cocked and ready. The sword at his waist on the left is so long that the scabbard drags behind him some on the sand. -- Several of the men notice and point. Their conversations go up a bit in volume but then stops when David hollers out.

"I can tell you this for shore! I ain't watching no torturing tonight! Not tonight! No sir! Matt - Jeff - ye'd best keep well back o these two here. And tell 'em all what I said just now. Make it plain."

Captain Chicken trots up fast.

"No, no, no, Davey, don't you get yourself all worked up like this. This is an Indian thing here. Let them handle it. They know what's what better 'en you son, believe me." David is shaking his head. Chicken sees it's about to get ugly and calls out for everybody.

"Hold on now! Jeff! Hold on. Ask em... ask em if they'd rather have it from big red here," Chicken points to David's sword. "Or a chance to show brave on the pole there. Go on."

Chicken nods at Jeff and then looks back at David. "Then you'll see what I mean. Ask 'em Jeff. Tell 'em they can pick - the pole over there - or the big red blade." He points again at David.

Jeff points to one old man, "That scalp's mine."

"Of course, Jeff - absolutely. He's your rightful bounty, no matter what."

Jeff then asks the first man and he wants the Cheney, speaking and nodding to the pole. The second man, the one Jeff took, says he wants Big Red. -- Jeff smiles and walks over to David.

"I say to him - if he kill you - he take big red and go - him free man."

David steps back a bit when Jeff is done - regretful - embarrassed. Matt walks up and takes the pistol David hands him. With another grimace he draws the blade out, takes a high guard and hollers, "Well tell im to come get it then!"

Then the sword is coming down on an old Tuscarora warrior bolting towards him - the sixth man David has killed in two days.

CHAPTER 6

DAVID FIRST ARRIVES IN THE INDIAN LAND

FOUR MONTHS EARLIER- SEPTEMBER 1712

The gulls cry out and look down at Matt and Jeff as they paddle David in a canoe from Port Royal to the Euhaw village. The trees are thick on both sides, green cypresses taking over the banks - with little beaches and sandy coves scattered along. A swineherd is making a ruckus on a beach up ahead. The mockingbirds and all the rest are singing their songs. The ring of insect chime is still very heavy - last days of summer.

"Damn, this here's some right smart travelling," David calls out. "I reckon we're making 10 knots - upriver at that! Or do the currents run backwards here?"

Jeff answers from the back, "We are Yamassee, sirrah. Tideriders." Jeff is short and stout, with long muscular arms and dark skin - a native born Yamasee.

David grins. "Tides ye say? -- Coastal ebbs and flows - caused by the moon?"

"No." Matt says from up front.

"The moon is over world - the waters below us, the underworld. You call it a river. Hey listen man - if you want to move righteous like on the water, then you got to know the tides. They bring the water in and out - in and out - everyday."

"Two times." Jeff is steady paddling.

"Just so. Twice a day. Are the waters not such in the World of Scots?"

"We have tides there, Matt - but nothing like this."

Matt nods and keeps on stroking.

"We paddle upriver when the tide is rising, easy, like now - and swoop downriver like the wind when the tide drops, eh?"

"Florida and back, many, many times - no problemo", Jeff adds. Matt nods again and keeps paddling, looking ahead.

"We wander where we want, me and Jeff, but mostly... mostly we just ride these here tides."

The two are steadily paddling up the Broad river. The wind and the tides are pushing them perfectly. David looks around in wonder at the expanse - water, blue skies and greenery all around.

"Ye fellers sure speak good English. I was told not to expect that, from the natives I mean, like yerselves." David's brogue is pretty thick.

"Did me uncle Raymond teach yer?"

They both shake their heads. "Nunh-unh." From Jeff.

"Well who then?"

Matt says, "You will see."

Matt spots some pigs up ahead and makes a sign to Jeff.

"Is Wright's land?"

Matt shakes his head. "Not this far up."

"Might be him sow."

"Might - might not. Let's go see."

Jeff eyes the canoe for space. "No problemo."

The hogs here is about to overrun us, as they is living high in the woods now - eating everything and loving them acorns especially. Snakes and such is just snacks to the big boars - and the sows gotta be watched close less they ruin our own corn. They leave in the morning and come back around evening time - for the most part, that is.

-- Shannon Carlton - 1705

CHAPTER 7

THREE LITTLE PIGS GET CHASED

The trio make the beach without being noticed by the swineherd. They crouch low and move quietly on the sandy soil, downwind of the pigs.

Matt and Jeff hit two little pigs with arrows from about 25 yards out and the shafts sink in deep, but the pigs still take off. -- David hits one with his fowling piece in the ass a split second later - #6 shot, and it runs off fast. All the rest scatter into the woods, including the sow.

Matt and Jeff start after their pigs and take them down after a short run. The arrows slow the pigs down considerably, catching up in the low brush. The tomahawks bring them to a short stop.

David starts to trot after the pig he shot, but the big sow turns and comes back for him. He fends her off with his gun barrel once, twice, but gets knocked over on the third try. He bounces up without the gun and runs for the nearest tree, jumps for a limb and swings up quick. The sow is a big one - well over 200 lbs.

Once David is settled up in the tree he is popped by a mockingbird on the back of the head, almost causing him to fall out. The sow looks up at him, snorts with a grin, then turns and trots off, stopping to root around some at the edge of the tree line.

Then the mockingbird dives on David again. He startles, swings out and down, catching another limb and loses his hat. He looks down at the hat falling onto the dirt - then up at the sow trotting away into the woods. Then he drops down, picks up his hat and gun and walks back to the river, turning around and watching as he goes, keeping an eye out for the big sow - and the mockingbird.

Matt and Jeff come back, each with a pig dragging along behind. They see David by the boat and Jeff shouts to him, "Where's you pig?"

David shouts back, "Gone!"

They pull the pigs into the river, where they start to float and get rinsed off some. Then Matt and Jeff lift them up by the legs - gently - places one towards the bow and one towards the stern. They settle David into the middle, climb in and start up the river again - still riding the tide.

Fresh Air is to be cherished, for it is the most important asset of a plantation community; as without the intake of constant and copious amounts of pleasant breathing none of us can thrive - neither master nor servant. And the air here - in the Carolinas - is most refreshing.

Clayton Grainger - 1707

CHAPTER 8

DAVID ARRIVES AT THE PARSONAGE

Matt and Jeff paddle David up to the parsonage, just across the creek from the Euhaw settlement, at about half past noon, and met by two widows under a portico that's just off the beach. -- The men hang the pigs up. The widows scrape the hairs off, then split them down the middle, and gather up the pluck into large metal pots.

The trio then go hang the pig carcasses in a little hut that's rigged up on the edge of the woods - just within sight of the house and portico. It is a bamboo frame structure under laid and overlaid thick with green pine boughs. David says, "I reckon this'll spoil right quick out here, what with no salt."

"Naah. These pine needles here'll keep it sweet. Get's a nice tang too after a while, eh?", Matt says. Jeff grunts and grins. "Course this'll all be gone afore Sunday. If it was high summer though - or say a real big ass boar - we'd smoke it some first - wrap it in palmetto leaves - then bank it in green pine boughs just like this. A layer of pine - then a layer of sand, eh?"

The aroma of pine needles is heavy, and their eyes are all watering as Matt expounds on the pine banking theory. "Works for sweet taters too. You can bank a lot of food here with pine boughs and sand, David - or dirt."

"Up ground," Jeff says. Matt nods, "Right. It needs to be well drained anywhere we bank it. Palmetto boughs is good too."

They head back to the portico, and see Pauline walking down from the bluff. She wears a short sleeved blouse showing off most of her arms; and light pants, a short mid-calf length, with ankle moccasins - all very stylish. Her hair is worn long and also partly up, with strings of beaded jewelry binding the patterns - very fanciful. David has never seen a woman in pants and is mesmerized.

"I'm Davey - Raymond's nephew..." Pauline frowns and cuts him off.

"No. You are not. Listen. The contraction 'I'm' signifies both a presumption on God and a certain lethargy in speech. And someone your age calling himself Davey, sir? A child's diminutive of the proper name? No." She looks him up and down. "You are done with diminutives here, sir. They call me Pauline and you shall be called David, a name with honor, meaning God's beloved."

David takes it all in pretty easy - smiles, "What does Pauline mean then, love?"

"It means very little actually, a feminine diminutive, as it were."

The view from the portico is both coastal and bucolic; with trees and shrubs and beaches surrounding a little house on top of a small bluff. The large fields of corn are further out, peas entwined on the stalks. Closer by are little gardens of squash and such, vines mostly - running up along trellises of bamboo, full of flowers and vegetables - greenery - and one tall trellis loaded with nothing but morning glories - the vines, the leaves, and the blossoms.

Across the creek and set back are smaller houses, not too close together - a house every 50 yards or so. All very neat looking with bamboo trellises here and there, also bearing vines.

The Mico paddles across with his sisters family and several canoes. He speaks a fair English. Matt sees them and calls out,

"Here comes the Mico."

"Bueno!" Pauline calls back.

The Bear clan Matron, who everyone calls Dona, climbs out at the bank and grabs up some baskets. "Hola Polina! Mira - de honey cake - y bread de corn - muy crispy - muy bueno."

"Hola Dona! Your timing is perfecto! Our drummers have just returned fully laden. Two pigs and one Scotsman, via England."

The Mico takes an interest then, "Engaland?", he asks.

Pauline nods," Yes, Johannion. Allow me to introduce to you Mr. David Kilbernie, the son of our dear Raymond's sister, Charlotte."

"And your passage David - how long wast thou under?"

David looks confused and turns to Pauline. "Your voyage David, the crossing. How long did it take you?"

"40 days and 40 nights, sir. (Shakes his head) Not a trip I'd care to take again."

The Mico nods and starts again, "My - nephe-eww, as you say, our Inacua - he travels under to the Engaland even now - as we speak. He carries our hope to your Queen. That we might keep the white ways, as we do with all the clans. He has the tongue of the Cherokee, the Sioux, the English, all our close friends. We hope your Queen to send one of her clan to here, for us - to learn the White ways. Say us David. Is your Queen a generous woman? A wise woman?"

David's eyes lift up at this, then says.

"I can only tell ye for sure that she is exceedingly fat, sir, and has to be carried about in a litter - or rolled along in a chair with wheels when she gets about - as she can'nae walk by herself." He shakes his head. "And I'm a Scot, sir, nae English."

"But you speak the English way. Is the tongue of the Scots

not the same?"

David frowns at this, "Well - most of the words are the same now, I grant ye. But the Scots way of talking is nae like that of an Englishman."

"Scots talk more big - make *big* farts", Jeff says and laughs and David laughs too. Then Matt puts in, "The Scots you can smell from a mile off, the English only half a mile or so." More laughs then - David and Pauline as well.

"The Scots are the patrimony, the English the matrix. Two parts of the whole that stand as one; as the Euhaw do with the ten towns." Pauline says as she looks to David. He stares back at her, mesmerized again.

The widows return and place baskets of fresh cooked meat, along with roasted sweet potatoes and squash, on a short bamboo table. Pauline finishes tea and brings it around. They already started with the corncakes, or fritters. All have a good time as the mockingbird looks away, back to the woods. The birds all still singing, and the insects still ringing their chime.

After dinner Pauline and David walk up to the parsonage - a big round Full Nut Moon just on the horizon. He looks at the bamboo trellises and flowers winding up in the moonlight. "This place is... I... I ain't never seen nothing like this Pauline. It's like a fantast. And I'd like to thank ye for the tea - the grand welcome, and all of that. I'm much obliged."

"Hah!" Pauline grins and starts an eye roll - stops. "Well! I am glad to receive you David. And obliged too, for what you did not do. Not taking offense at my earlier remonstrance, on our first meeting no less." She shakes her head. "I... It caught me unprepared. Your arrival, I mean. I was away on my rounds when word came that you were in Port Royal. And Mattias, he did well to bring you at once; but I had not the time to prepare for it - not properly." She takes a few steps away, then one more onto the little porch and lifts her arms up.

"So. Here stands the parsonage built by the right Reverend Raymond Bray - your uncle, David." He's staring and she's looking him in the eye. "He has appointed me his subaltern here, and, as it were, de facto mistress of this place." She smiles again. "Your arrival has long been anticipated, David."

Pauline steps back down and takes his arm in hers - then gestures with a wave. "I make no introductions of you to Ma'am Persimmon, nor to Ma'am Sassafras. They are both widows of the Yamasee, and sisters. Their way is Bear Clan. They are employed here as seamstresses, and also as our most able cooks, as you have well sensed, eh?" She stops and turns to look at him face to face again.

"We are all here, and I include you now, David, we are employed in the work of the Society for the Propagation of the Gospel to Foreign Lands, an Anglican ministry. You do understand me?" David nods back to her. "I do not introduce you to them as their command of English is well, non-existent. They could nae comprehend yer speech at all, David, eh? But they do know your name, and know that you are beloved of Raymond, our minister, and his favored sister's son. They will assume you the Inacua, or Prince... the heir apparent."

"I'm not his heir."

"Well... that remains to be seen."

CHAPTER 9

DAVID LEARNS ABOUT THE WHITE DRINK

On the morning after his arrival, David and Pauline look out across the creek at the men gathered around the lodge. Pauline points over and says.

"They drink the Cassin, a blackish tea with a white froth, and smoke the pipe all morning, every morning, weather permitting. Telling stories of their raiding, or their dreams perhaps, until they can smoke and drink it no more." She's nodding her head, and then looks to David.

"Then they go off and purge themselves a while. It is supposed to make them more pure, more like the way of the sky, the wind, less the way of the flesh; parted from time. That is the best I can explain it to you David."

"They take the leaves of a prickly bush, a Holly your people call it, and boil it until it makes a strong tea. I've tried it myself and the taste is horrible, muy bitter. I grant that it is an excellent emetic, but how it transports one into the wind is beyond my ken." She looks at him with a wry smirk that he learns about soon enough, and then continues.

"It is rather like rum in some respects I think, what with the drinking, the smoking, the bragging, then the puking their guts up. Rum is noisier though, and messier, no doubt."

"Whatever they's drinking, love, it ain't nothing like rum, nothing. That's plain enough to see. Why... they's just sitting about there like wee lords, having themselves a smoke. Looks peaceful enough to me." David's looking over at them, not at her.

"What's an emetic?"

Pauline looks around and waves, calls out, "Yoo Hoo - Jeffery! -- Come here, dear one."

Jeff has been watching from the woods nearby - inconspicuously he thought. Anyway, he steps out and walks over quick.

"David wants to try the black drink."

"Nooo... Por Que?" Jeff frowns and shakes his head.

David asks again, "What's an emetic?"

"Go and learn for yourself." Pauline looks at Jeff and says, "One cup for him Jeffery, and no more." Jeff shakes his head, looks at David. Pauline prompts them again.

"Go on now. Let Jeffery introduce you to the men. Do what he says and share a cup with them; if you can stand it. It is a purgative as well as an emetic."

"Purgative?"

"Try it and you will see." He's looking doubtful now - not so sure about crossing over with Jeff. Pauline sees that, smiles and says, "You will be fine David. Just maybe not drink the whole thing, eh? Spill a little bit first."

They paddle over to the men lounging about bare chest and barefoot - rubbing bear grease on themselves. David asks, "What's that stuff they rubbing on themselves - some kind a grease?" -- Jeff says, "Bear grease."

And then a little while later on the mockingbird gets very interested in David, as he is vomiting up a storm in the woods, retching loud and stumbling - and cursing most vociferously too, between the bouts.

He recovers a bit and walks some more, looking around. The

Mockingbird - Bluejays - Cardinals and a Red Fox - all are looking back at him.

He stops and vomits some more, then in a grimace "OH shit, shit, shit, no!" -- He takes off his belt and pants and stepping behind a tree wails.

"Hell no, no, no, never, never, never again ...."

The mockingbird takes off then, with the birds singing and the chime of insects all around. The fox sticks around, still watching - captivated by David's antics.

CHAPTER 10

THE FIRST OF THE MALADIES DAVID IS SPARED

David turns out early the next morning with no shirt on and a buckskin wrap around his loins - like the men at the lodge - like Matt and Jeff walking with him.

Pauline takes an astonished look and stares - then calls out.

"Hoy! David, Jeffery, Mattias - hold up! " Then she trots up quickly.

"No, no, no, I think not. Ye want to be roasted alive, like green corn come noon, sir? No! Ye are a Scot and ye must dress as a Scot here." She's shaking her head and taking a deep breath.

"Listen well to me now David." Pauline points to the north. "Your uncle Raymond, when he last wrote to me, he stated, 'Endeavor Pauline, to spare him of the maladies common to this place, as you know them best. Instruct him to listen well to you first on all the ways of survival here, as it is a most perilous place to the uninitiated.' That is what he wrote to me David. So! The first malady you shall be spared from is a bad sunburn."

David is taken aback a bit and blurts, "What?"

"Go put some clothes on David. Then you and I shall take a little walk, eh?" She says, hands on hips - elbows out.

The forests about this place is filled with Cattle, some's mine and some's me neighbors - we's got em branded so to tell em all apart. -- They just wander loose here, the weather being such as it is - no black frosts really. The husbandmen need not bother with their care at all - except for the making of a Cowpen, for the newborn calves in their season. -- The steers from these flocks are slaughtered twice a year - pickled in barrels and shipped to the Barbados and Sugar Islands - so that the Englishmen there need not lack for their beef.

-- Maria Carlton - 1709

CHAPTER 11

DAVID LEARNS ABOUT THE BERRIES, JOHN WRIGHT AND SASSAFRAS

Pauline and David wander the edge of the woods and brush nearby - just within sight of the parsonage. She instructs him on the plants. Mockingbirds, robins, bluejays, redheaded woodpeckers, cardinals, and more are singing from the trees nearby. She's picking berries and gathering a few herbs - speaking to her companion along and along.

"These are rabbiteye, and edible." She holds up one close to David. "See the eyelashes of the rabbit? Very pretty, no? Yet all the pretty berries here are not so good to eat David. In fact, some can make you very sick. And some can kill you. Right quick too." David starts to pick some berries.

"No, no. Do not pick. Not yet, por favor." She shakes her head and laughs. "Before one gathers one shouldst make sure there are no spiders underneath, eh? And no three leaf." She chuckles some more then stands up straight.

"Please, David. Touch nothing about you for right now. Not with your hands, at least. Just walk with me. And talk with me. About whatever you like. Look for rabbiteyes too, any berries, you let me know. And watch out for climbing vines - especially those with three leaves." She swings the basket to him. "Here, try some. The darkest ones are the sweetest."

He takes one from the basket and chews - makes a face. "Not bad really - a bit like a sour grape." Pauline laughs. "We have those as well. You will like these better cooked." They walk on a for a bit.

"Ah! Here is the three leaf." She points. "That little vine there can raise nasty welts all over your body, David. Any part of the skin it touches will make for a blistering and painfully itching sore. Get it in the wrong places, sir," Pauline says, eyebrows raised, "And you will never forget it. I have seen some scars last years. It is a most pernicious weed too, very hard to kill. Remember it. Note the leaves of three, David, and let them be."

They walk on some more and David says, "It looks a bit like English ivy to me."

"Ivy is decorative, and a darker green. That back there is poison."

Birdsong aplenty still - but there is a definite lull in the insect chime.

"And here we have pokeberries. Very pretty - no? Some birds eat them, but they are not for the people, David. That cluster there, if you were to eat all of it, might mean the death of you." She's nodding with a grimace directed his way.

"And it can give you a skin rash too. So again, do not touch - comprende?" He nods and walks on along with her.

"Ah - ha! Here is the fly catcher. Watch." Pauline points down and David is intrigued as he sees one close on a fly.

"What do they want with flies?"

"Good question... but I do not think it wants anything." She reaches down and takes a pine straw. "Here, tickle the insides. The little hairs, with this, gently."

He feathers it across the top and sees the action. "Is it poisonous too?"

Pauline chuckles at this, shakes her head. "No. They are a danger only to bugs. They consume insects but do not move otherwise. So... are they flora or fauna?"

"Fauna?" David guesses. Pauline smiles as she straightens up.

"It is a cherished medicinal herb, David. Especially so for women. Those who are pregnant with child. And it is good for coughs and chills too, of any sort." They continue walking along the edge of the woods.

"And here is the pinesap." She pries away a bit of sap from a pine tree with her knife. "The Queen's navy depends on this now you know, for pitch and tar, and turpentine. From these trees here, we use the sap mostly just to start our cookfires. "

"And some of the people there", Pauline points across the creek, "boil the turpentine out. But the tar and pitch making... Well! I liken that to getting a foretaste of hell David. It is the nastiest of smokes. And forbidden in Euhaw. If they want to make tar then they got to go away, way off. And downwind too."

David chuckles at this. "Well I've worked some smudge pots, love - and they ain't near as bad as the smoke from a foundry."

"Foundry? What is that?"

"It's where they make the metal, love - the works. The smoke there - and the heat - well, it sticks with a body, like a fever." He remembers back to his short time of trying to make a living as a workingman - on wages, and shakes his head.

"Smudge pots ain't nothing really. They stink some sure - just stay upwind is all. But a foundry ...well... imagine a smudge pot as big as a house - and a fire so hot that it melts the pot."

"You speak in jest, sir. A riddle of some kind? A fire that melts the pot?"

David pauses here a bit and thinks some more - holds a hand up. "A forge has brick walls. A special made brick, Pauline, that can withstand a heat that melts iron. The Hardwick foundry had five big blast furnaces going when I was there - 12 feet high and 5 feet across - each one as big as yon parsonage there."

"What can be hotter than a tar fire?"

"They burn coal there, love - not wood. -- Charcoal burns hotter than just wood right? Quicker. That's how they finish dressing the buck skins here - with charcoal?" He nods and she nods back. "Well, raw coal - coke - it burns a lot hotter than charcoal. And it don't come from no trees neither. It's mined out of the hills back home." He looks around. "Y'ere not likely to find any hereabouts. The land here is too flat." He turns back to Pauline and shakes his head again.

"I cannae explain it to ye any better than that, love. I worked there for a bit - til one day I just said to hell with this shit - quit and never went back." He grins and snorts. Pauline frowns, then sees something and motions him to be quiet.

John Wright sails up the creek with a piragua, four boatmen, and David's boxes.

Pauline sees Matt and Jeff walking up, and deftly leads David away - further into the woods.

John Wright climbs down off the boat and wades in from knee deep water, reaches the beach; then calls out, "Matt and Jeff - just the fellers I was hoping to see. Have you seen any strangers about recently?"

They stare back like statues, saying nothing. Wright continues on towards them and out of the water, "Well.... might I inquire then as to mistress Pauline's health - or her whereabouts, then?"

Jeff says, "She is about her business, sirrah."

Matt says, "Doing her mission work, as she always does, sir. And she is in very good health. But what of you, Mr. Wright? Has the season been agreeable to you - doing well yourself?"

Wright smiles and says, "I have been doing well, Matt - very well indeed. Penned five new calves of late, and got sign of four more. Busy man me, eh?" He pauses here. "There is this one little queer thing that's happened recently - found one of my pigs a couple days back. Had to run a wolf off him I did - but it ware'nt no wolf what killed him, no! -- Care to guess what it was?"

Matt and Jeff say nothing - statues again. Then Wright pulls out some lead shot wrapped in a kerchief - opens it and shows them the pellets.

"That right there peppered up the whole of one ham and rurnt near all the bacon! That and the wolf anyways. -- Well... I never saw such a thing in all my borned days." Wright gives an animated and astounded look at the pair, with both of them still like statues - not deigning to do more than glance at the pellets.

"And then I wondered, who amongst all of the peoples hereabouts - who was even likely to own any bird shot - much less waste number 6 on a wee pig. And then I looked at them boxes yonder." Wright points to his piragua.

"Me and Jeff don't shoot no birds."

"Yamasee waste no powder, sirrah!" Jeff starts walking around - making space.

"No man here has wasted any kind of shot - not of late anyhow - and none have taken game within your purlieu, sir."

Wright is intrigued. "Purlie-uu? What's that Matt?" Matt does not answer. Wright continues on," So.... have ye seen any of me cows on your rounds?"

Jeff snorts, "Damn cows." -- Matt says, "We've seen sign aplenty, Mr. Wright. They's eating good enough I reckon - now that they's found all the deer trails. Huh! Aint' hardly worth our time even checking em now, as all we see is cow sign. -- No deer sign at all."

"Not mine surely - not less'n they've swum the Broad River."

"No - not yours, I reckon." Matt frowns. Jeff turns and heads up to the house, leaving Matt alone with Wright.

"So, Mattias - are ye acquainted with our visitor here - a Mr. David Kilbernie?"

"I have made his acquaintance."

"Where is he?"

"He is with Pauline, I assume."

"You assume, eh?" Wright smiles at this. "Tell me Matt, what are you doing here amongst these folk? You with no wife, and no clan neither. I cannot help but wonder it."

"I live here because I like it here, sir. The air is good. Suits me very well - and the food's even better - despite there being no deer."

Wright chuckles again at this. "I could use a man like you Matt. And not for labor neither - but as my foreman. Mine's a getting on up in years now - and malaria's eaten into his liver I fear - not fit to do much more now than help me reckon with my accounts."

"Accounts? What is accounts?"

The mockingbird is watching Pauline and David walk the edge of the woods.

"I think that's the boat with my goods on it." David says.

"Let the porters tend to it then. Twill be there when we get back." Pauline frowns and lifts up her sap basket. "You know, this sap here would not be so necessary to us; if John Wright had not cut down all the Sassafras."

"Sassafras?"

"Yes. Sassafras; a tree. The big leaves make a fine tea. The tender leaves are edible, good for stews. We made teas from the roots to stop diarrhea, and the inner bark lining made a good tea for the cramps. And from that bark we also made tinctures and salves for bug bites, and potions of all sorts. A blessing it was to us, David. It used to be."

"What are ye talking about?"

"Trees, David." Pauline spreads her arms over her head. "Trees that grew 40 feet tall. Medicine, shade, food. But the best thing was the wood itself."

"It catches fire quickly and burns well. A hotter fire as you say, eh? An acceleration of the combustion. We had Sassafras in abundance when I was growing up here, David. Many, many stands. And then John Wright came and cut them all down. We have had the worse for it ever since."

"What - I mean - why?"

Pauline's frown turns to a smirk. "Why do you think, sir? Pounds sterling. What else? The English use it as a cure all of sorts, I have read, much the same as the people do... or we did." She is mad now - ready to curse but catches herself and takes a deep breath.

"And he was not content just to cut it down from his own lands. No, David! He led a cooperative effort here. All the English. And all the clans too; the men at least. And now the Sassafras are gone, David. Gone! Just like the Deer."

"Damn his eyes!" David curses, ever ready.

Pauline shakes her head and looks away - and a forlorn look it is now.

"May be," she says. "But everything takes longer to cook now, thanks to the senior John Wright. And I have to gather pinesap everyday now, for which I thank the Good God for, but it is not the same, David. Not the same at all."

At the Parsonage
Jeff, David, Pauline, Matt

CHAPTER 12

BOOKS AND MUSIC

At the trellis portico - birds chirping - a couple hummingbirds just hanging out.

Pauline asks, "David, do you read Latin?"

"Not so's you'd know it love."

"Now what does that mean?" She asks, quickly exasperated.

David thinks a second and says, "It means ... I know the letters and I know some words - but to read a text - no."

"Well.... that is better than no Latin, I guess. There are many expressions, in Latin, in the books here, the bibliographies, that I do not understand. Raymond saw fit not to teach me any of that before he left."

"No Latin?" he asks.

"None", she says.

"Show me one of these books."

"I can show you all just as easily as one. Walk with me."

Pauline leads David to the little library building and asks, "David, did you by chance happen to bring any books with you, on your rather arduous journey across the Atlantic?" She has a mischievous grin on her face.

David hesitates, says, "Uh... No?"

"That was an equivocal response David. Are you quite sure?"

"Equivocal?"

"It sounded like you were asking me. And you hesitated."

David shakes his head and says, "Sorry, Pauline - I didn't pack no books - no."

"Did someone compose your letters to Raymond for you?"

David shakes his head - smiles. "No. Those were all in my own hand, love."

"That sounds unequivocal, good (nods). Please make certain in your words here David. It *is* important." She turns and looks away.

"I have some musical compositions though", David says. "Not a book - but it's something to read - sort of - and the citterns too."

Pauline turns back to him, clearly interested again. "Citterns?" she asks. "And compositions?"

David smiles. "Be easier to show ye, love." They turn around and head back to the house - leaving the books for another time.

Pauline, and now David live in a Creek style home, but larger. It is rectangular in shape - with two layers of bamboo for the exterior walls. The ceiling is slightly pitched to the middle. The center beam on top is pine - and there are two posts of pine inside to support that beam. One post is almost hidden by a tight lattice of palm fronds wound through, screening off about 1/3 of the house - Pauline's room. To enter she just eases through one of the frond sections, in their middles. The rest is open except for the widows' work table and two chairs - with shirts and skirts and pants, and a couple of cloaks and quilts stacked on the table. Pots and pans and tools are hanging on the walls.

They un-box the instruments and strings - wrapped in silk and surrounded in cedar chips and rushes - moisture control. Along with some clothes - wool pants and sweaters - a heavy overcoat, to which David points to and says:

"They assured me I would never need these clothes here, but I brought em anyway - for padding if nothing else, right?"

The smaller heavy box has 50 shovel blades - 50 hoe blades - 50 finished trade knives. -- The last box is long, and thin, a planked wood and extra sturdy - opened up it holds two pistols - a matched pair. And a jeweled twin edged dagger with a matching two handed long sword - red rubies in the hilts - Damascus blades both.

"These were me da's. This is what I have left of 'im."

"This... this is beautiful." Pauline touches the flat of the blade. "What is this pattern? An etching?"

"No. It's called Damascus - a special way to make metal that I cannae make nor explain to ye. Forged steel and well polished though - not an etching."

Pauline holds up a pack of strings. "And these? These are strings for the cittern, eh?"

David nods and wonders if she's seen Raymond play, "Yes - ye see it has eight strings - but they are in pairs - so it's just four courses. The bass strings are copper core - wound with strands of brass. And the treble strings - those are special. High nickel steel wire - pulled in gauges from 18 to 10 - made in Spain."

"Gauges, David? A measure?"

"Yes - this 14 gauge here - that's 14 thousandths of an inch thick. Easier to say gauge than thousandths of an inch, right?" He smiles. "I've 200 of those - and 200 of the brass in various sizes - gifted me by uncle, as an incentive to depart from England see, and spread music throughout the Carolinas."

"Did he give you the knives and hoes too?"

"No - those I bought with me own money. Raymond sent a list of goods he thought worth the shipping cost - and these particular implements packed easy - stacked ye see. He asked for hoes and shovels, and I got them at a good price. I figured I could trade the knives and just keep the shovels mostly - ceptin what we need here ,right? Til I see Raymond anyways. What d'ye think?"

Pauline stares at the goods for a bit, nodding, then turns back to David, "Raymond wrote to me that you had a dispute in Wales - with a magistrate."

David frowns. "Right - that shitfart. And it were the magistrates son - not the magistrate. -- Fonvielle... Fonny we called him - the son of a bitch."

"David! Please! Do the telling without all your derogatory invective!"

David scowls and looks down and then back up to Pauline.

"All right - he and me - Fonny, we were good buds up until - up until he lost his head one day and slapped some poor wee wench silly! Knocked er over he did - and then the son of a ...." David stops before cursing again.

"He started back like he was going to put the boots to her, he did. Which I had seen him do a many a time afore - on fellers what was just asking for it. But on her? No!" He shakes his head and looks down. "So, I shoves em off her and he pitches out on his arse. Then I asks him - Ye want a taste o my boots now - ye little shit!?" David pauses and looks up at Pauline, who nods back, like go on.

"So Fonny... he pops up... his mouth just a spewing out with derogatory invective - which I need not repeat now. Well... I had to do a bit more work on him then convincing him, right? (Headshake) Then - when we'd finished with the matter, or so I thought - instead of me a leaving him there a wallering in the mud for anybody to roll out... I put him back up on his fine red stallion - got him back to his stable - and handed the reins over to the groom."

"The next morning the Sheriff's at my door - first thing - says you got to come with me now lad. To where? I says, knowing - and he says - to the castle."

"I says you can leave here well astride yer horse sir, or not - but ye ain't leaving here with me. Go and see the Lord Henry's barrister - a Mr. John Holt, and apprise him of yer warrant - if ye have one. -- Well... he goes all red in the face - starts to say something - then backs up and walks away - gets up on his horse and trots off." -- David looks away to the East - remembering for a few seconds his past life - the second son of a Baron.

"What happened then?

"Nothing - or well - everything I guess. -- I came here - eventually. -- The sheriff did not come back. But I'd already had some trouble. All the magistrates and sheriffs knew me there - in the Weal and back home too. -- I didn't inherit see - and me brother Robert already has three sons, God bless 'em."

"And if truth be told me ma wanted me gone - as did 'er new husband, right?" David looks away - East again. "So me and uncle, we came to an agreement of sorts. He handed me a pamphlet of the Carolinas, written by an Indian Agent here, a Scotsman name of Nairne, though he claims to be a Swiss in his pamphlet - with a name like Nairne too. Huh! Anyway, he went on and on like it was God's gift to the Commonwealth - a paradise on earth, land free for the taking - with no taxes neither - not for lands nor goods. "

"So, here I am, right? And now glad of it. This place is like a paradise! The air here is... it's just - it's sweet to breathe here, Pauline. And there ain't no brawlin' nor fussin' here - no English fart curling his fat lip up at me. To hell with 'em!"

"David!"

"They ain't none likely to miss me back there in the Weal, love - ye can rest assured o' that."

Pauline looks at him closely now. "Why d'ye keep calling me

love?"

"It's just an expression - and I believe I just caught ye in a contraction there love." He says and smiles at her.

"What else do you believe?"

-

David picks up the big cittern then. As he tunes it he hums the note first and twists the peg until it matches. Pauline watches him, and there's a smaller one that only has four strings on it.

"This one here's a mandore." He says.

"Mandoray?"

David nods, "It's derived from an ancient eastern instrument - called an Oud. The Marmadukes first brought 'em to Spain, somewhere around the 12th century, and then the old el oud became the new lute," he laughs.

"Anyway - it's me apprentices attempt. Neckjoint warn't tight enough. Put 10 strings on it and it bends the top down like a bow too, but with just four strings on it she plays well enough. Rather have four good metal strings anyway than 10 made of sheep gut, right?" He hands it to Pauline. "Try it. It's tuned like this'n here - just four strings instead of eight."

She plucks it some - looks up smiling - then picks out a little melody using just the top and bottom strings and it sounds pretty good. David asks her, "Ye've played before, then, right?" She does not answer, but just keeps playing. David watches her patiently, listening close now to the tune.

When she's finished he says, "You know you can tune it differently right - use different size strings? Me music master Patrick, he said the sounds of the strings are not bound by our imagination. They simply await our discovery." He's smiling big now. "I thought he was talking about the different boxes back then, with their different kinds of wood having different tones. Back then I thought that - but now I'm thinking he meant the tunings too."

"Is this what King David played?"

"No - that was more like a harp, I think - a wee bit one. Raymond could tell ye more I'm sure."

"And what is a harp?"

David looks down, ponders. "It's got strings - lots more than the cittern here (thumps the body - bump, bump) - and no frets (points out the frets) - and no box to amplify the sound see (taps the body a few more times). It's different. It has a sweeter sound. More... complex. I don't know how else to tell ye. I like it, but they're hard to learn. I can draw ye a picture if ye like?"

"Why... yes. Yes. I should like that very much."

"Play that little ditty again - what ye just did. That was pretty good, especially for a first go. Let's see if ye can do it again."

Pauline smiles and plays it again.

It has at last been enacted by the Commons House Assembly; all lands bounded to the north by the Combohee river, and all the isles of the south by the marshes and islands on Coosaw and Port Royal rivers, and all the land south to the Savanna river - indeed all of the choicest parcels surrounding Port Royal have been set aside for the exclusive use of the Yamasees, who have been our most stout defenders against the Spanish of late. Now every white man who has staked a claim there in amongst all those choice pieces - many of which were already cleared and drained by the Coosaw. Why, they'll have to give it all up now and go cut trees somewhere else. All excepting the minister, of course - his church and glebe lands and the school house for the mistress there - that can stay. But the rest - they got to clear out. Hah! Ye should have heard John Wright a cursing Nairne. They've boxed him in good now.

-- Clayton Grainger, on the Act, No. 271, that granted the Yamasee their lands in 1707

CHAPTER 13

TIME FOR SCHOOL

On the next morning David prepares to go with Pauline in her little canoe to cross the creek.

Pauline says, "Today is school day here in Euhaw. A special day too."

"Why's that?"

"Here in Euhaw I teach English and Mathematics; both a primary and secondary form. At Cheechesee, Okati, Pocotaligo and Altamaha I have just the primary. "

"Sarah and Rachel, my secondary students here, they both read and speak English very well now, and they understand more than just their sums. So today I want to talk to them about Euclid; Geometry, and the use of ink on paper, as it applies to both Geometry, and to our letters of course. So... I should like a little extra help from you today, David. What say you?"

"If it is within my power, mistress, then I am at your service."

Pauline makes a petit frown, "You do qualify a lot of your statements, sir."

"What?" He says back. She smiles and nods him up to the front of the boat. She pushes them off and they start paddling, cruising up the waterway easy. Pauline calls out "Escuela mes amis! -- Schooltime little deers!", to the houses and people as they pass, two times up and down the creek. Turning to the Euhaw bank David jumps out and pulls the canoe aground, where Pauline is quickly surrounded by six girls, some calling her mother - some Paulina. She collects herbs from the children and two of the mothers who are attending.

Pauline chats with them all, then offers out a basket of honey coated chestnuts, which get taken and eaten - the gift exchange. They talk in Creek for a while. The girls tell where they have found new herbs - the mothers nod. One asks for garlic and Pauline nods.

"Sarah has found spiderweed on the Reorsha creek - in the shade and with the green flowers - as you like it. She wouldn't let me pick it though." (Laughter)

"Goodness." Pauline grins at Sarah and then to the mother, says, "She did well then. The petals must be fresh for the cure to work. Is it right at the water?"

The women shake their heads.

"The flowers need water mixed with your urine now; some everyday that it does not rain, if possible. Ten parts of water to one part of urine. And poke holes in the ground there around the base - at least one hand out and point it at the roots - enough so that your water does not run off. Pour it out easy and let that water seep in good."

Sarah's mother asks, "Sweet water?"

"No. Water from the creek is fine."

"Kind of salty there." Another mother says.

"A little bit of salt will not hurt. Only water it on days it does not rain. Or water it just before a rain, if you can. But not just after a rain, eh?"

Pauline switches to English. "Pay attention now little dears. Today the secondary class shall start on the Geometry of Euclid. And the use of ink on paper. Writing." The girls murmur and look at Sarah and Rachel.

"You, David... you shall hold the primary class here. Count with these little dears the count."

David's eyes pop open big. "The count?"

Pauline smiles, "You do know the count David? 1, 2, 3,4... (holding up her fingers - while the little girls giggle a bit) Lead the count with them, in numbers as far you like."

David is smiling now too. "Ye want me to scratch some numbers in the sand? Have 'em copy em' out?"

"Yes, David. An excellent suggestion; do just that. And then do the same with the alphabet. As a call / response lesson; and scratching the letters in the sand as you say. And then have them spell words too - like deer - or wolf - or cittern, which they do not know yet, of course."

"Have them spell any word you like, but explain it to them first, eh?" She looks across the creek and nods, "We shall be just up the bluff there, at the library." She turns to the youngest ones.

"Little deers - this is David, as you all know. -- David, this is... (four Indian names that David does not comprehend - girls are young, 7 to 11 and have not taken Christian names.) Pauline continues, "David is here to call the count and the letters with you. Then, a writing lesson, of sorts." She smiles and nods to them. "Listen well to him my little deers." She turns away with Sarah & Rachel climbing in the boat first and then she pushes off, paddling back to the parsonage.

David says, "Well - I guess, (raises a hand) One _ Two _ Three"

The girls answer in unison up to 10. David says, "Alright then... let's draw some numbers (makes a slash in the sand). That's a one - who wants to go first?"

The oldest girl takes the stick and draws two through ten while the girls make the count again - not in unison anymore but some kind of weird bright song tune. When they're done David is astounded, and whoops out.

"Whoo-eee! Can y'all do that again?"

The oldest girl nods and says, "We can go on all day. The numbers never end you know."

"Well... I have heard that but never tried it out."

"The letters have an end though. They number 26 - both in English and in Latin."

"Oh yes - that I ken."

"But the letters en Espanol number only 24. Why is that, David?"

David thinks a bit. "That I do not know, love - I can speak a little Spanish - a little bit of French - even some Gaelic - but English is the only language I really know. And Pauline is somewhat skeptical on me ability there."

"Paulina can teach you. She knows all the languages - excepting Latin", oldest girl says to him - very earnest.

"That's good to know, love. Ye want to go on with the lessons yerself for a bit, then? -- Suits me fine just to watch. Ye'd be learning me how to teach, right?"

The oldest girl nods and starts the Alphabet call / response.

CHAPTER 14

WHERE DAVID LEARNS HOW TO BE CARGO

Pauline walks to the beach with David. It's early morning and there is a touch of chill in the air now. She is wearing a cloak, long pants and a buckskin skirt - all of her solo long paddle gear. She waves and calls out, "Jeffery! Yoo hoo! Wait up dear one!" Then speaking to David, "Mattias and Jeffery will acquaint you with their rounds this morning. I shall travel in your wake until we make the river and then ride the tide up to Pocotaligo." She stops and takes his hand and looks him in the eye.

"Listen well to me now, David. You are not to go off on your own; not by any means. Not yet. The land here can be treacherous. Any newcomer can lose his way here, and turn up as meat for wolves and buzzards. Should that be your end David - a thing gnawed on by beasts? No." She shakes her head and points over. "So, Mattias or Jeffery - or myself shall accompany you always in the Indian Lands. In any of your gettings about. Those men there know the lay of the land here, and you should avail yourself of their ken. They are our drummers, and a right fine smart pair, eh? What do you think?" He nods and looks over.

"So listen to them David. And if you don't know... don't go. Ask someone first, eh? Take the time to learn this land, and learn it well... before you get all caught up in its wanderlust."

Pauline heads over to her little slough boat. David watches her walk away.

Jeff says to David, "You see de canoe - is a two man canoe - three man - you - is cargo. Good thing about cargo is - it keep still - so you (points) - keep still."

"You's the passenger man", Matt says, "ain't gotta work for the ride, so just relax and enjoy the scenery. But don't move none in the boat. And don't talk. Point to some deer if you see some - or hogs - but most of all you just need to keep still - so as your movements don't throw us off our stroke, eh?"

"I gotcha."

CHAPTER 15

THE CEREMONY OF THE HARVEST

The Harvest Dances are in early fall. David knows it is a big festival but is forbidden to attend. He sulks about it and sneaks up on the first day anyway. He watches them dancing from afar. Then the mockingbird gets curious and flies over - just the women - doing the Ribbon Dance - fascinating.

But before all this - back at the parsonage, David pleads with Pauline, "If I take the black tea can I go?"

"No. You will remain here and do as you please David. Except no shooting. Plenty enough here to keep you busy for a few days."

"Days? Why cain't I come and just watch? I won't say nothing less'n ye tell me to." Pauline shakes her head.

"Yes, no, and no. I can fain look after you and tend to my work. Listen to me, now, David. This is a clan affair, and you are... well ... not of the clans. You are a friend of the people, but nae one of the people - comprende?"

"And the first day is just for the women; the planters ceremony. The second day is just the men; the hunters dances, lots of those." She rolls her eyes a bit and smirks.

"I may come check on you then. Or one of us will." She takes his right hand in her left, and with her right gently tilts his head up - looks him in the eyes.

"The Harvest ceremony is a very solemn thing David, a ritual; that must be done only the one way." She shakes her head slowly and caresses the back of his head with her palm and says, "It would leave you bewildered at best. You can take care of yourself here for a few days. I shall ask the clans about inviting you for the last day, the feast day. It is a more relaxed affair then. The dances then are not so ... ritualized. The women and the men can dance together then, eh?"

CHAPTER 16

DAVID NEEDS A BATH

On the last day of the Harvest festival David is allowed to attend - where he runs off from Pauline's fairly innocuous advances and suggestions.

It starts off back at the parsonage, as David sees Pauline approaching.

"Hola David!" She calls, "Have you missed me?"

"Hola yerself - and Yes! -- I have missed ye - missed everybody - even the widows. It's so quiet here I can hear the foxes pissing in the woods."

"Hah! So, did you continue with the black tea?"

"No. Ye didn't tell me to - did ye?"

"It matters not." Pauline chuckles. "You have appetite enough, surely."

"The clans are all agreed to welcome you to the feast today. But we shall have to get you cleaned up good first, eh? And I mean a thorough scrubbing David. With lots of soap and the rag, all over. Not that hop in and out rinse you call a bath. In fact, you should just let me attend to it. No time like the present, eh?"

"I know how to wash meself!"

"Ye have not proven it unto me sir," she laughs. "All of my senses note otherwise." Pauline twitches her nose. "Some more so than others."

CHAPTER 17

THE HARVEST DANCE

David and Pauline arrive at the feast - on the beach, where there is plenty of food and fun. Some girls practice their English with David, and he nods and answers - calls them all love, but does not linger with any. Pauline watches him as she walks over.

"So when do the dances start?" he asks, "I don't know any of the steps."

"At dusk. Give all this food a chance to settle." Pauline pats her stomach. "We shall watch the first dances together you and I. See if you can catch the rhythm (shakes her hips a little) - so to speak."

When it gets dark there is indeed some spirited dancing and singing.

"This is a call response song David." She wraps his arm in hers. "Like most of them. Here the Mico calls out... and now the response from the women."

"Note the movements carefully. It is absent of any pattern, no? Unrestrained, yet bounded by the rhythm. As the night goes on the beats and the tones will fluctuate (here she swings her hips fast then slow) - but it is mostly as you see now - the men and the women dancing together - around and around the fire."

They dance on the beach. -- Pauline is wearing tight knee pants and a form fitting broad cloth top - short sleeved - all the other unmarried girls dress similarly - some with short cloth skirts - and all of them have their hair down.

The married women dress differently, with their hair still up in partial buns - standing far outside the circle - wearing their cloaks for warmth. These matrons are all very well dressed, talking amongst themselves and pointing.

It is apparent as the dance goes on that some pairs are missing in the circle. Pauline detaches from the bunch and looks around for David - curious. She trots towards the bluff for a bit and stops - sees him walking back to the parsonage.

CHAPTER 18

PADDLING DOWN TO OKATI

Pauline is always busy, with gathering and sorting well integrated into her teaching agenda, and the women who help support her know that they can count on her for clothing and medicine. The widows make enough blouses and pants to clothe all the Euhaw matrons - and most of Okati too.

So Pauline offers gifts wherever she goes. Sometimes honey coated chestnuts - always herbs and medicines and garlic - sometimes berries in baskets - and sometimes clothing. And she spends a lot of time listening to the children, gathering their stories as she does the herbs and roots.

The matrons of Euhaw give Pauline the best of their comestibles, so that she and the widows never lack. And David helps her prepare for her daytrips, away from Euhaw.

At the beach one fine sunny morning, Pauline and David are walking to her little slough boat.

"Jeffery tells me you have learned a fair enough stroke on the water," Pauline says - looking at David's arms.

David frowns, "First I heard of it. He calls me 'cargo' and 'keep still' mostly."

Pauline chuckles, "Well that is when you are in the middle, eh? What does he say when you have the bow?"

"Dereche y Izquierdo. -- Right and Left."

"Come on with me then today, paddler. We can make Okati before the turn if we put our backs into it. Got you a kit packed?"

"Up there", David nods to the parsonage. "Let me fetch my

long gun."

"No!" She shakes her head. "If the men see that piece they will want it bad. All of them, David. Trouble I do not need. This is not a hunting trip."

"Me knife then?"

"Yes of course, but just the one. This is not a trading trip either, David", she says flatly. "I have an extra waterskin but bring your canteen. And your hat."

They load up - paddle with the sun on their backs and a smooth steady stroke and moving fast. There is a slight chop on the waves from the wind at their backs - and the tide too, is helping them along. They make the beach at Okati and it's still early morning - a blue sky up above and the waters flashing all around them.

CHAPTER 19

DAVID STIRS UP THE PEOPLE

"Hola Paulina!" -- "Hola Dona!" Pauline is talking with the women and children - doling out honey coated chestnuts and busy with the gift exchange. -- David has some toddler boys and girls climbing up on his legs - a few older girls want to touch his hair. Hair that's getting a bit long now, too. He is surrounded by whimsies of all kinds. Pauline looks over and lets them be.

David is passive and smiling - catching one boy before he trips - easing their hands away from his genitals. He tries to talk with them some. "Any of y'all speak English? -- No? Easy there now lad, don't hurt yerself." Then he sees the older boys on the chunkey field - watches their game - studies it a bit. -- When Pauline is not looking he trots on over to the field and asks if he can give it a try - motioning with his hands to one of the boys - who hands his spear to him.

He then throws the spear ahead of the ball while it is rolling, and the ball rolls into the spear and bounces off - a feat which causes a bunch of whoops from the boys. More come over and David tries it again and this time hits the ball while it is rolling. Lots more whoops then - including some men.

Everyone now is interested. Pauline sees it finally and makes a face; both grim and a bit anxious. She starts over to the field with the rest of the people. They all converge on David.

"They want you to try it again", Pauline says, "but this time throw it where you think the ball will stop rolling. That is the way of the game, eh?"

"I did not know that, love - maybe I should just watch these lads here now for a bit - learn the proper way of it."

"I think that is for the best."

David is smiling, "Well I only hit the one, right?"

Pauline looks at him and frowns.

CHAPTER 20

A PROPENSITY FOR VULGARITY

On the paddle back from Okati, David tells Pauline about his martial training.

"I've had lots of practice love, with everything. Javelins, spears - halberds, pikes - daggers, short swords, long swords - you name it - with mail or without - on horseback or afoot. -- The short javelins I had were very much like that Iads back there, right. -- I watched him for a bit, and well .... his spear was a good'n - looked to me to be straight and true."

"You might not have liked it so much had you caught them at the ball game." Pauline is smirking now.

"What's the ball game?"

"They make two sides, four to a team; and they knock the chunkey up and down the field with sticks."

"Chunkey?"

"The ball, David. And they strike that ball most violently, and each other too sometimes, with the sticks, up and down the field." She's paddling steady.

"There are posts on each end. Did you not see them?"

David says, "Yeah - I saw em."

"Well... the team that knocks the chunkey onto the other teams post first is the winner."

"How big a sticks?"

"Not that big, David. Smaller than the javelins, as you call them. The chunkey is used to train the boys for fighting. And fighting on the run. The ballgame tests their endurance and speed; their skill in striking, and their tolerance for pain. They mostly show restraint mind you, fending each other off with their sticks instead of knocking heads. But I did treat one boy who was blinded in his left eye. Inshumaya, he's called now, or one eye."

"What happened to him?"

"He went on as before, onto the warriors way, a man with his own wife and clan now."

"What happened to the other boy - the one who hit him?"

"Oh! You would not want to know all of that." She stops paddling.

"Tell me anyway."

"Well... The warriors all praised his skills after that, David; night and day they did. Told him how strong and how powerful he showed himself to be, in blinding his enemy." Pauline shakes her head and frowns.

"I heard he left the people then, and did a long, long time in the wilderness. Not just a night or two, but many, many moons; on his spirit way. When he came back though he got himself a name; Wolf Watcher. He told the people that the Pater and the Mater of wolves were the only ones who ever took down deer. Said the rest just trailed along and got something to eat when they brought them down. Mater was the fastest and tripped up the deer, and it was Pater who trailed her and made the kills, mostly... but it was always the Mater that tripped them up first, he said." She has a big smirk now.

"He must have been an exceptionally fast runner to have witnessed such things, eh? He married into Wolf clan right after that. Spends his time hunting them now instead of watching, I suppose."

"Wolves?", he asks, and Pauline says, "Yes, of course."

"Why would he do that? There's no market for wolfskins - and ye cain't eat wolf. What's the profit?"

Pauline laughs a bit at that. "Wolf clan eats wolves David. And they wear the fur in wintertime, as do many of the people. Why else call them Wolf clan?"

David paddles on for a bit and says, "Huh! Well... I never heard of such a thing. Eating wolves. ------- How many clans are they?"

Pauline frowns, then says sourly, "Perhaps this is a lesson you should learn on your own, David."

David persists though, "Did ye say they praised him?"

Pauline stops paddling again. "Oh yes, yes indeed. Bragged on and on about his strength and cunning. I just saw the start of it and I was busy. Saved an eye but not its vision, eh?" She starts to paddle and stops again. "Listen well to me now David. Have you noticed a propensity for vulgarity in my speech? Any heretofore, I mean?

David is paddling along, "Uhhh... no. Your speech has been completely un-vulgar like, I'd say."

"You stay away from that bloody chunkey, then! You hear me, David? It is not for you!" She picks up her paddle and practices breathing for a bit - watching his back - he keeps on paddling.

CHAPTER 21

GEMI TEASES PAULINE ABOUT DAVID

Pauline is in her canoe coasting up onto Pocotaligo - the Big Town.

Gemi, who is also a greens woman and clan leader, waves to Pauline.

They call out greetings "Hola Polina" - "Hola Gemi" - then speak in Creek.

Gemi: I heard you found another man on your travels - a white one this time. -- How many is this now? And where do you keep them all, dear?

Pauline: Hah! Found him? More like he was delivered to me - like a babe he is too - have to keep a close watch on him.

Gemi: How close now? -- Come on dear one - tell me all about him.

Pauline: Well... not that close - got to finish raising him first, eh? Like a big babe he is, tossed into the wilderness. And put upon me because no one else wanted him, it seems. (Gemi is laughing now) -- I have grown rather fond of him though. But he will not be my babe much longer, I think. He is headed north soon, with all the rest of them.

Gemi: Again? (Astonished contempt)

Pauline: Again. (Resigned frown)

Gemi: (Pauses and looks around - thinks) The Tuscuraora are weak now. They will go to the Five Nations.

Pauline: (Shakes her head) They will stay and fight. They

shamed Colonel Barnwell last time, if truth be told. -- He could not take that fort, Gemi, not even close. -- But a fort won't save them again. The Cherokee have sent 400 fighters down they say, all looking for bounty. And the Sioux are all painted up again as well. If the Five Nations of the Iroqouis do not come down soon the Tuscarora will be wiped away.

CHAPTER 22

ABOUT THE YAMASEES REALLY BIG CANNON IN ALTAMAHA

The Euhaw warriors paddle in 10 canoes down to the large town of Altamaha - where David sees women wearing cloth skirts - but no blouses - just a cowl over their left shoulder which leaves their right breasts exposed. He is amazed by this and asks Matt, "Do all the women dress like this - half naked?"

"What you see is the traditional Yamasee dress - sort of anyway." Matt grins.

"But they're half-naked!" David says again.

Matt chuckles, "Come back in summertime - then you can see the other half."

"They don't wear nothing?"

"A little moss skirt covering their bottoms - but nothing up top. -- Gets pretty hot here in the summer, bud. You will see."

"But - the women in Euhaw. They all had clothes on." David's staring still.

Matt thinks about this a bit. "Well... that's Pauline of course, from her ma, eh? Christian modesty and such? You'd have to ask her. Me - I try not to get Pauline going about the Good Book - nor any book for that matter. You know how she is."

"Damn!"

Matt laughs again some then says, "The clans in Euhaw - they all look to her first. But here - here they got they own ways."

David and Matt take a tour around the lodge house - and then up the little bluff where they see the Mico standing beside the Giant Alarum Cannon.

David is amazed yet again. "What the... ? Where did this come from?"

He hears then the tale of the giant cannon, as Matt translates.

Matt / Mico: This is a gift to the Yamasee from the Government - to sound the Alarum should any hostiles arrive - Spanish - or anyone else making the red path onto the people - or our English friends.

"Have they ever fired it?"

Mico / Matt (smiling): No - the Yamasee have treaties with the Creek - the Cherokee - the Catawba - all the people who ride the tides. From Florida in the South to Cape Fear in the North, they all are bound in the white way with us, the Yamasee. -- We have no need for an Alarum. No clans make trouble for the Ten Towns - nor for our English friends.

David listens and nods - understanding.

CHAPTER 23

FOUR POUNDS STERLING FOR EVERY SCALP

The gulls sail overhead as a big piragua boat pulls close onto the bank. David sees John Wright Junior, first one off the boat - jumping into the water, splashing up to beach and grasping Matt and Jeff both saying:

"I hope you fellas is ready! -- We's headed north on the tides, brothers - Government's just raised the bounty on scalps. Four pounds current money for every head now. Whooeee! -- We got 40 muskets in them sacks yonder!" He points. Matt and Jeff and Junior whoop it up again, as others join in.

CHAPTER 24

WHERE JOHN WRIGHT FINALLY CATCHES UP WITH DAVID

Matt, Jeff, David and Junior and a few others are hanging out on the beach. Junior asks one of them, "Why you quit with the "scoutboats"?" He asks it in the Creek language. The other man, a Yamasee answers, "The whites all treat me like shit - better to leave than to have trouble - especially stupid wolf trouble."

Junior, whose mother was from Wolf clan, takes offense and shoves him on the shoulder a couple times "Call me wolf again puta - puta." -- Matt and Jeff back off a little bit.

David understands little Creek but does not like Junior's tone and says, "Hey! Leave im be now."

Junior turns to him and points. "Mind your own damn business, sirrah. -- Do you know what he just called me!"

"Don't know and don't care. Just leave im be."

John Wright Junior stares at David and walks slowly up to him - then nods his head like he's going to pass by and at the last instant whips around with a big roundhouse left, which David blocks with his right and comes with a hard straight left of his own and all his shoulder behind it too. It knocks Junior off his feet and onto the sand. -- Then he scrambles over and rolls up - a bit wobbly. He looks at David - gives a war cry and closes with him fast but gets knocked down again; a hard straight right this time.

Junior scrambles over - gets back up and makes a running leap at David and then they grapple together - falling to the sand and wrestling for position. Junior takes an opportunity while they are lying together sideways to get in a few licks at David - trying to box an ear - gouge an eye. But then David turns him and gets on top - lifts up a bit and goes down hard with a knee into Junior's solar plexus, who goes limp and stops fighting.

David stands up and Junior turns on his side moaning - clutching his stomach.

Forty yards off and up the bluff there is a big, fat white man striding towards them. -- David watches, and figures that it's the elder John Wright.

John Wright walks up fast and stops about 10 feet away.

"Ah - here is the man himself - and just the one I've been looking for too this many a day. Ye've been squirreled up in the Indian Lands more than two months now hain't ye, Mr. Kilbernie? And not a one o yer neighbors has so much as laid an eye on ye now, has they? Much less had a proper introduction, eh? -- The man's a ghost I figured, a phantom, a fault of hearsay. Yet here ye stand in the flesh before me... after all of my searching and inquiries. God's to figure."

David is non-plussed and asks, "And yer name sir?"

"My name, sir, is John Wright and you are David Kilbernie. -- I own the land around that big red bluff ye passed back coming up this way - not five miles back. And it was my piragua, sir, what sailed up with your boxes and delivered them safely unto the parsonage door. " He cocks his head a little and continues.

"So - ye appear healthy, hale and full of piss. How is it that ye have not yet applied for your warrant, sir? Nor made your proper enrollment in the militia?"

David is a bit wide eyed now and somewhat caught out by the sheer torrent of words and replies.

"That warrant for 100 acres can wait till I'm ready to claim it - Mister Wright - and it'd be out by me Uncle Raymond's land anyway most like. When I can get around to it that is. I hain't been out there yet so there's no use for me to bond out a plat for it in Charleston. And I would a come in for the militia - if I'd a knowed of it - but it's like ye said, sir. Hain't a white man laid eye on me since I got here in the Indian Lands sir, not until today. And I thank ye, sir, for delivering my goods safely." David looks over and points, "Can I presume that yonder vessel is yours?"

Wright turns and says, "Yes it is - the 'Quince Ano' - and it can travel any river hereabouts with a draft of three foot - less sometimes, if not fully loaded."

Johnboy moans and turns over again sitting up. David looks at him and then back to the elder Wright, "And that's yer son there?" It looks like another fight stirring in his eyes.

"Now, now, Mr. Kilbernie, not to worry," as Wright holds his hands up, "Not about knocking John Junior over anyways - no. -- It's a good thing he finally got a proper lesson in fisticuffs. Had it coming to him quite some time now, didn't he?"

"You see, the natives here don't make a proper fist - no - so Anglish lads like John Junior there can give them a licking anytime they like." He shakes his head.

"What they don't know is that them bucks is a way better off for it, eh? Not busting up their knuckles over nuttin - wasteful like. No! If it's time for blows with them lads - then it's time for tomahawks, Mister Kilbernie - 'nae' fists."

"Ye ain't no scot - not with a name like Wright."

John Wright smiles at this. "Well I've been around a plenty o Scots - and that's the truth. And I cain't remember a one I dinnae like neither. -- The best folks I ever knew was Scots, in fact. I say knew - because most of them are dead now."

"Listen here, since ye brought it up. I had a home and a thriving business in Stuarts Town - a Scottish town - here in the Carolinas - once upon a time - before the Creeks burned it. -- I was the blacksmith there see - went from prentice to journeyman to shop owner, when old man Exleigh died - in the space of just two years. Had the shop in me own name when I turned 21 - and had a couple of apprentices working for me too. Then Colonel Armstead shows up one day and asks me how long it would take me to make 100 Carolina trade knives, just the blades - no handles. I looked at the blade he had there and said maybe a week if I had another good smith working with me - but as all I had was me indentured lads it would be a fortnight, possibly more. Then I thought about it some and told him if he could have the pig iron and charcoal delivered to my forge I'd guarantee 14 days - from that time."

"He agreed to that, and a few days later I received all the pig and charcoal necessary for the task. A trader was with the Colonel see, and he got the charcoal from the Cusabo - and a 10% interest in the number of knives produced."

"Well ... The Colonel had collected over 1200 lbs of pig - a busted cannon - old anchors - pieces of cannonballs - all sorts of crap - the detritus of war, eh?"

"Anyway - I made the 100 knives in 10 days, got paid in Spanish silver dollars too, not no public receiver notes. And I had metal enough left over for five hundred more blades. Or hoes - whatever I wanted."

" I raised my oldest apprentice to journeyman not long after that. He was fresh off the boat, but he'd done some farrier work back in Burnside and made for a quick learner. " Wright turns and looks off into the south, remembering.

"Then along and along after that I left him there to run me shop, so's he could get a start on earning his own money, see. That's when I started out traveling with wares of me own then, trading with the locals - all the Indians here."

"I was away then - on one of me trading rounds - when

the Creeks and them Spanish devils took Stuarts Town. They destroyed it all - burned the whole bloody town down to the ground. I'd've hardly been able to make out where me own shop sat except they left me anvil there - couldn't claim that now could they? Haul away an anvil? I reckon not." Wright shakes his head.

Well... on that day, however, I was sailing past that big red bluff back there ye passed coming up the Broad river. Ye've seen my lands, sir?"

"I've seen 'em."

"Good - so you know who I am. Now as to why I have been looking for you, it is to propose to you a Coronet's commission in the militia - for the upcoming campaign on the Tuscarora."

David steps back, cocks his head, asks "And why should ye do such a thing?"

"That is a question best answered by Captain George Chicken, who would be your commanding officer should ye decide to take the commission. -- Ye're here with them Euhaw bucks right? Well, we got a special task set for that bunch."

David thinks a second, then asks, "Where is this captain?"

"C'mon with me. We're a meeting in the longhouse." They start walking together. " And how is mistress Bray these days? I trust she is in good health?"

David keeps walking and replies brusquely, "I don't expect she'd want me to tell ye much about her business. (Stops) Why do ye call her mistress *Bray*?"

Wright stops too and turns to him and says, "Because that is her name sir - recorded on the register of births in Charles Town - in the year of our Lord 1694 - Pauline Bray."

"Who's her da, then? Me uncle Raymond?"

John waddles in a little closer to David with his biggest smile.

"No - she was not sired by yer uncle, sir - nor by any of 'us Scots'."

"How d'ye know this?"

"Because I sold her mother to yer uncle, did I not? -- Got her in a raid down St Augustine way. And weren't it meself what dragged her out of the Alcalde's house - after I shot at him first that is."

"Pauline was his get most like - favors him some she does." Wright nods his head a bit and pauses, makes a knowing smile.

"And you know, I remember very well the day that she was born too. I was at the parsonage see - made camp there on my way to Pocotaligo - as I often did then. There were no Euhaw across the creek neither - not back then. Anyway... Raymond comes out to me all smiling and happy - says Donna's just had a babe. A girl - and one that she's had some great vision about too - something about the Apostle Paul and... well...I don't know what all. But he was real happy - only time I'd ever seen the man smile, I'm sure." Then Wright steps in bit closer - within arm's length now and continues on with his smile.

"But listen here... Pauline... she warn't Raymond's. I can guarantee you that much at least, Mister Kilbernie."

David looks a mix of relieved, then worried again. "What happened to her ma?"

"That I do not know sir. Perhaps she is buried under one of the parsonages eaves - as that is the way of the people here. They bury their dead next to their houses - close by, eh?"

"You don't know how she died then?

"No. I do not. But Pauline, well she's turned out as fine a lass as any man could ever want, don't ye think? None smarter - not that I've seen - and not just in them Injun ways - that herbal lore they set such store in - but book smart too. Sharp as a tack that one. She'd make a fine catch for any enterprising young man wanting to improve himself - guaranteed. My Johnny is quite enchanted with her, and can't say's I blame him neither, eh? Not a shilling to her name mind you, but she runs that town there right smart, don't she?"

"They all know her name here - all the tribes - even to the Chickasaw. She's big medicine, lad - big medicine. C'mon with me now - let's go hear what the Captain has to say."

CHAPTER 25

DAVID SIGNS UP FOR THE MILITIA

When David and John Wright go into the longhouse, the Micos are sitting along their benches with the war leaders and some more fighters. There's one white man in the midst, Captain Chicken, and he calls out.

"Come join us my friends. It's time to smoke the pipe and make some plans. John, I assume this is the man?"

"Yes George - I have the rare pleasure to introduce to you mister David Kilbernie, the nephew of Reverend Raymond Bray, who is currently residing up along the fall line - near the Seraws."

"Good. I'm George Chicken, David - glad to make your acquaintance. I am the Captain of the Broad River militia, and have your enrollment papers set here before us. I have a special job for you sir, an offer for a coronets commission and pay - and an opportunity to make some bounty money - all while going up to see your uncle, Raymond Bray. When have you last spoken to him?"

"With Raymond?" David asks.

"Yes man, who else?"

"I hain't never seen him - not that I remember anyways - much less spoke to him. -- We have corresponded often enough this past year though."

"Well.... I should like you sir, to take a message to him. You and the Euhaws will take the bounty offer over to the bucks of the Santee - Wateree - and the Cheraw - and try to discover from them any possible water route to get from the Cheraw country over to, or above, the Tuscarora lands - or some path with an easy portage. If so, you are to take said route and make a reconnaissance of the Tuscarora country. Chart any fortifications - towns - settlements - anything of interest that you see along the way. It's not a fighting mission - take scalps if necessary - but take no captures en route. Your job is to keep these bucks moving David - offering the bounty - and scouting the territory. -- If there is no water route available then you are to make haste back downriver and rendezvous with my Catawba fighters on the Onslow somewhere. Jeff or Matt know where it is - lots of little coves there. You will all have to look to your own provisions en route too - for most of it anyway. All your fighters will receive a musket with sufficient ball and powder for the duration. And a coronets pay is 5 pounds per month. So... what say you Mr. Kilbernie? Will ye take the task?

"Do you have a ready map of our route here - for me to take with me?"

"Yes. Up unto the fall line at least."

David nods his head - slowly - then asks, "Gold Guineas? Or current paper guarantees?"

"It is in paper sir - plus whatever bounties you can acquire."

"And how long do ye expect this campaign to last - a year?"

Chicken pauses, "Oh... that is hard to say for certain - but figure a year - more or less."

"And what are the likely prospects for bounty?"

"I claimed four captures last year - good ones too - all quite lively. A tough bunch they was, to make it back here alive."

"How much did that fetch ye - in current money?"

"Not a cent, sir. I took two twenty guinea gold pieces for the lot. And they probably sold for twice that in Barbados."

David thinks some here - takes his time and says, "I am willing to go on this expedition for ye sir, but if I'm to receive only paper guarantees in recompense - it will have to be on the double. -- The money here is worth only half a proper guinea - at most. Not something I could take back home and spend in the shops now, is it? So, if ye want me to go upriver - it's 60 pounds - upfront."

John Wright explodes, "Ye're mad laddie - 60 pounds upfront?!"

David stays calm and says, "Yes. And I'm not mad. There's no guarantee that I'll make it back here to collect any pay right? -- And no provisioning other than powder and lead? -- And ye want me to paddle up and down the whole of the wilderness from here to Virginia and back for 5 pounds a month? Whoooooee! No." He shakes his head." "60 pounds upfront sirs, and send it to Pauline Bray. Give her a little cushion while me and the drummers is away."

"She don't need no help there sir," Wright says, "That woman looks to herself well as anybody - believe me!"

David is firm and says coolly, "Nevertheless - she will have the notes."

Chicken is frowning. "We don't have such on us."

"I'll take your promise then, for its delivery to her sirs, as quick as humanly possible. And she can do with it as she sees fit. And Mr. Wright?"

"Yes?"

"Take the widows some pigs along and along while I'm gone."

Wright smiles at this and says, "I should be glad to visit with Mistress Pauline in your absence, sir."

"Just leave the pigs with the widows sir. And have one of them Euhaw women there fetch her from the woods back o the house when ye take her the money. She don't want ever to see ye nor speak to ye again - but she'll come if ye tell em about the notes. And that ye have a letter from me."

"We'd have to take this to the assembly, sir", says Chicken.

"No. -- Mr. Wright can guarantee it here and now. Ye can get that money back from the assembly sir, at yer leisure."

"And why should I bother with such a convoluted - and troublesome exchange?"

"Just do it - take her the money and the pigs - just little ones - easier to hang up." David smirks. "And if ye can by some means manage to bring her some sassafras seedlings, sir - maybe holler it out first upon yer arrival, ye might catch a word with her yerself. Otherwise - don't bother yerself with her no more."

Wright scowls bad at the last bit of the transaction and says, "All right then. I shall request that the assembly make an advance of 60 pounds for this mission. If they don't reimburse it, it's on me."

"And the pigs, sir." David importunes.

"Yes, and the bloody pigs too." Wright snorts and struggles to stand up. David pops up and lends him a hand.

CHAPTER 26

IS THIS REALLY A WAR?

Matt and David sit looking out on the water at dusk.

"Are we really going to fight a war?" David asks. -- "I mean - with these piece of shit muskets here? Like, actually go attack some fort up the coast - Matt?"

Matt stares off into the distance a bit, then turns, "Listen David - me and Jeff - you know what we do right? We are the drummers - the scouts - for the Euhaw - for all the people - understand? (David nods) -- We check this place out here - everyday - and we bring back game for the people. Just us, or the other drummers - from the ten towns. No one else needs to be up on our deer trails around town ceptin us - me and Jeff, and now you. We look for sign - sign of game - sign of clans on the move - or the Spanish. -- Any signs of movement in the area - you understand? (David nods again) -- We see some now and again."

"Spanish?"

"No, not of late - but we do see signs of war bands on the move sometimes. So we follow them to see who they are."

"Who do you follow?"

Matt chuckles some. "Well we don't know until we catch 'em now do we? It's Seneca and Tuscarora mostly - or used to be. But they don't wander much down here along the Broad river - not no more anyhow."

"Why's that?"

"Cause the Yamasee ride the tides like el Derecho, brother. --

Once you see us it's too late - way too late."

"What the hell does that mean Matt?"

"It means they's done if we see 'em brother!" He laughs ironically for one so young. "Like the steers in autumn, ready for slaughter."

"That's nonsense - y'all ain't cannibals."

Matt stops laughing now. "Well - depends on who you ask now, eh?"

"Listen here, David. This is the way of it. We give those folks that we catch to the traders - maybe keep some little ones if the women want. Then the traders 'give' us pots and pans - guns and knives - all them clothes and pretty beads on the women you see here - where do you think all that shit comes from?"

"Pauline has the widows make clothes for them."

Matt nods and says, "That's right - but just clothes - and she 'gives' them all away - and so the people 'give' to her everything she wants too. We don't get much deer now - but she don't lack for rabbit, nor fish, nor cornbread - nor them herbs she grinds up for teas and what all. It's women stuff man. But that ain't us - not me and Jeff."

"We chase people David. Hunt them down - catch em and kill em! Or sell em. And we're good at it - real good. Maybe because we've been caught and sold too - way back - but that shit don't happen no more - not to the people. You ain't seen any wandering clans around here have you?" David shakes his head and Matt goes on, "Cause they know. They all know. They call us derecho malo - bad thunderstorm - the one that wipes them out."

David mulls and sulls on this, "Well.. it's got to be better than listening to Pauline's harangues all day. Don't do this - don't touch that - stay where I can see you - go help the widows - find something useful to do. Sheesh!"

Matt looks at him dumbfounded now - truly astounded.

"Man - that's just Pauline trying to keep you alive. She's telling you what's what so's you can make it here, brother." Matt smirks and gives a small head shake and says, "Hey I know you want her, eh? She's righteous, ain't she? Better than all your Guineas, all your guns. You see that - dontcha?"

David says not a word - looks steady back at Matt.

"Listen David. Pauline's a woman - and she wants what women want right?"

David smirks back. "And what pray tell is that, Matt?"

"A baby man! I mean ... you ain't been helping her out none there now have you? I mean... Is they something wrong with you brother?" Matt snorts.

"No."

"Ain't it both of you living there in the same house? And you don't even try?"

"Try what Matt?"

"She wants some girls of her own man. Little Paulinas to raise up - right?" Matt shakes his head.

"But you'd best watch out for her David - and I mean this now. Don't you be like the rest of these English with they womenfolk."

"I'm a Scot."

Matt nods and closes his eyes a couple seconds and says, "Right - and since you're also our Coronet now too I think your first duty ought to be - you go make peace with Johnboy, eh? It's a mighty long way to paddle holding a grudge."

David is taken aback by this too. "Ye want me to ask John Juniors forgiveness?"

"I wouldn't put it like that. Just go talk to him - tell him that you know he's a fighter now, got heart and all - that you're glad he's got your back - no hard feelings, eh? You do that - and you'll feel a lot better about paddling up north with him at your backside for the next two months."

"Two months to Raymond's?"

"Not shore, maybe less, and it's mostly upriver, bud. But that's just getting there - wherever the hell it is all we're going *this* time!" Matt draws a deep breath and says.

"Man - I ain't looking forward to this shit here. Not one bit. -- See, I spent all last winter up there and only took one scalp. He was big medicine mind you - a giant covered in four bearskins if you can believe that shit. He was all shot through in his arms and legs from all of us at the end - like a bigass porcupine. And I took him down. But that was it, David. Aside from some few skins - all I got for purt near a year's work, brother! One single scalp!" Matt makes a grimace.

"And Barnwell even took my musket back after all that! Militia property, he said. -- So... a season of paddling - a season on the march - and two failed attempts to take that bloody fort. Huh! Well... I can think of better things to do than wander from here to Bath and Catechna and back - again! But ain't nobody here wants to hear what I think, David. We's a white town and we got to go fight when the red towns say so." Matt shakes his head and frowns some more. "Anyway... it takes longer getting back than it does just getting there - you can count on that shit."

"Be good to finally meet my Uncle Raymond - he's a reverend you know?"

"I do know that - now about Johnboy..."

"He was startin' trouble - asking for it."

Matt smirks at this, "Yeah - I reckon you can see that Johnboy is half Indian, eh? His ma was sister to the Mico in Altamaha. Not the man you met, but his uncle before that - that's the way of

cuddle in their nests in pairs - keeping warm.

"This Warr upon the Westos was done entirely without our approval or knowledge, sirs. We have learned of late that ye fought them not for the preservation of the Province, but so that those men of trade amongst your very midst, could gain an advantage, by extirpating said Westos - murdering the husbands to take their wives and children - and then selling those poor souls for specie - waging destruction and fire upon them who were in solemn treaty with you. Ye have induced the Savannah with promises of your guns, shot, and powder to make war upon your neighbor."

-- Lords Proprietors letter of complaint to the Carolina Grand Council, about their conducting an unauthorized war on the Westos - circa 1682

CHAPTER 28

DAVID MEETS HIS UNCLE RAYMOND

David, Matt and Jeff reach Raymond's settlement - one big log cabin - one extra large barn - several thatched Indian dwellings. Trees all around - folks with young ones about - doing their chores.

Raymond comes out of the house and is unarmed. A couple of big Indians are back about 50 yards right and left, lounging almost, but holding muskets with the muzzles down. There is a small crowd of people between the house and the well, and a couple at the turnstile - hauling up water. All of them are stopped in their routines and gazing at David, Matt and Jeff.

David hollers out, "Uncle Raymond - Raymond Bray?" He waves his arm in a hallo. "It's me - David. David Kilbernie, your nephew." He stops and lowers his voice some now that they are closer. "I got your letters."

Raymond stops and says, "Hah -- I thought it was your da for just a second there. New better as soon as I thought it and heard you though. I've been expecting you some time now. Well... you can call me Ray, son."

David says, "Uhhh - a woman I know - back at your parsonage - she reckons we ought to use our proper names - all the time - for clarity and ..... well ... they was other reasons she gave too. So... Raymond? What does that name mean?"

"It means protector - or watchman. Same as William - but that's German. Raymond is French in origin." He smiles at David and chuckles.

So... Pauline's been at you too, eh? Well.... let's get on in and have us some tea then - or some cider if you prefer it. You can call me whatever you like, David." He looks over. "Now - who's these proud looking mates you have here with you?"

David turns, "This is Mattias. This is Jeffery. They both speak English."

"God help us - but don't we all now." Raymond turns and heads to the house. On the way in he speaks again without turning around.

"I know why you're here. That Quaker gom - up the coast. Heathens and dissenters - criminals and worse - the whole lot of them." He stops walking and spins around quick and says, "Listen well now to me David. There is no chance of me or any of mine getting involved in any of that shit up the coast, eh? Are we clear on that?" He's staring David in the eye - very close now. Raymond is a big man - bearded and grey and hardened from his work; the constant clearing of new land.

"If you don't talk about the Tuscaroras, then you're welcome to stay - as long as you like - but not one word about them troubles up north now, you hear me?

"Uncle - I brought ye... brought ye some strings for your cittern."

Raymond gives an astonished, happy smile. "Well, God bless you son."

-

Later on they are well into the cider drinking and still outside. Raymond asks "How's that cider?"

"I thought it was ale", David says.

"Well?"

"The best I ever had - and the first decent drink I've had in I don't know when - no counting that cloudy swill in Charleston.

Port Royal's shit ale was even worse.

"Know what this is?"

"No - Apples maybe? Or some kind of young wine?"

"Not far off I guess David. But it's corn mostly - with wild grapes and berries - goosefoot weed - peaches - anything over ripe we have to spare. And July mixes in some honey too, I think - he don't tell me what all. But it seems to keep us happy and healthy - and ready for a little music most fine evenings - like tonight."

"Where's he gone to?"

"Tuning up the cittern - and his banjo - away from all this clatter."

David smiles, "Pauline plays one now pretty fair, ye know - a little four string I gave 'er." He takes another drink. "Did she ever play yers?"

"No. That was one thing of mine she did not get, neither her, nor Donna."

David is feeling the cider good now and keeps smiling, "Well... she played a pretty fair tune first time I saw her get a hold of one - made me wonder it did. And... she told me to tell 'you' that she wanted a Latin grammar book - and that if it that was too costly - that 'you, yourself' might scribe out a short primer for her on the next correspondence - 200 nouns and 100 verbs, she said - that should suffice to start with."

Raymond laughs now. "That sounds just like her - and that's her look too, son." He closes his eyes for a bit and smiles. "Of course she's wanting more books - always has."

"Yeah."

"She was a voracious little reader David. Just devoured our library by the time she was 10 - memorized it almost - criticizing one tract for faulty logic - correcting grammar in all of them. And she trailed me about with questions too. About Ann Hutchison - Queen Elizabeth - Queen Anne - St Augustine - fermentation. Once she learned a word she wanted to know all about it. All about it - like Jesus and the wedding wines."

"Fermentation?"

Raymond nods, "Yes, I couldn't keep up with all what she wanted to know - told her to have patience and trust in the Lord and that he could unfold all things to her in time, if she was earnest and followed in the way. -- She looked at me real hard one time I said that - asked me if that was the truth - 'Is that God's promise to me then - to have answers as to *all* my soul inquires?' Well - I marveled at that, even then. God knows what she's like now. -- I told her it sounded like a good idea to me - if you can think to ask it of the Lord, why shouldn't he answer you I said - and I said the same thing to her a many a time after that."

"What happened to her ma, uncle?"

Raymond looks down for a bit ...."Well her ma, Donna - God rest her soul - well... she just passed on - malaria most like. It caught up to her, like it does a lot of folk here." He looks down and shakes his head.

"I knew Pauline had to keep busy then so I gave her my little slew boat, made for me special by a carpenter back in Port Royal - named Bellamy. The bottom had an excellent finish - tough - and slick as I don't know what. Said he put 22 coats of varnish on it. I gave that to her and put into her care almost everything else I got from the Society. Ye've seen it."

"I tasked her to spread the word of God to the ten towns, and to see to the women what needed help with their babes and such, like her ma used to do. Teach them English, I said - teach them their sums - and any what was ready, start them on the Catechism. -- She'd take off for days at a time after that, then show up with a young'un in the boat like as not - her frail ones she called them. The stories she could tell about them towns."

"So why'd ye leave her there?"

"Oh she was ready for it - the mission I mean. And I had my land grant from the Lords to attend to here - couldn't be put off forever could it? It was all well enough off in her hands anyway, son. Any converts made there were entirely due to her - or her mother."

"She was 14."

Raymond pauses, "Well, 14 here is not the same as it is back home... A gal of age here can do pretty much as she wants. And by 14 she's a member of the clan - ready for marriage - although they usually spend some time playing the field, so to speak, like you rowdy lads." He looks down and shakes his head. "You've learned of course that it's the women here what run these towns? They wear the britches, so to speak. And it's them what's most like to repeat the words of the Gospel to their own girls later on, eh? -- That is the propagation here, David. They hear the word of God. They understand it, and they repeat it to their girls."

"The men now, well ... that is a whole different story. They got their own ways. And ye're as like to change one of them from their ways as a you are to tame a cougar. Have you seen a cougar yet?"

"No - I've seen the tracks - a big cat."

"As big as a man, he is, and twice as fast. Can take down a deer just like that." Raymond swipes his hand in front quick - like a cat's paw.

"Uncle......I um..."

"No! Now don't start that. I know why ye've come. After all this time, and not to see your long lost kin - no. Nor plot your warrant - but to round up some Seraw bucks to finish up that bloody business up the coast. Is that not the case? But that's not going to work here see and I can tell you why, son.

It is because the Seraws are mightily dissatisfied with the way Barnwell treated them last year - mightily so. And there's also been bad trouble of late too with the trader here, one Richard Cartrette." Raymond is shaking his head and staring at David; very animated now.

"He actually threatened to take the Mico's young ones for non-payment of debts - said it right in front of his bucks he did! Them all having a smoke at the lodge, relaxing, and he blunders in there with his blather - all for money."

"And that is madness, son! Bloody madness! The Mico said he had gone wolf and was no longer a man." Raymond shakes his head sadly and continues.

"Well.... that about sums it up David. The Seraw don't want to spend another winter on the hunt for the Government. This year they just want to go and hunt for food. Meat. And if the traders don't want the skins then they'll take them up to the Choctaw, and get French goods for them - or just do without." He looks earnestly at David with a plea in his eyes now.

"You understand there is no real law out here in the wilderness, eh, David? And the men here, they have been living outside the law, some for a generation now. All of them answering to no one. No mind for God, nor King, nor Conscience - doing as they please. They are not pirates per se, nor thieves - but rather speculators in piracy and thievery, kidnapping and murder. They are the very meanest sort of man, you understand me? And they are all about us now, David. Them and the heathens. Have ye met any? Any traders I mean?"

"Just John Wright - downriver of the parsonage."

Raymond smiles, remembering, "Of course you have - him I know well. He's the exception what proves the rule, eh? He does not cheat on his trades. And he has a fair enough education - blacksmith too. And John's done with the trade from what I hear, now that Nairne's took over as Agent again."

David says, "Killed his wife didn't he? And she was Yamasee."

"Yes I know that story. But before that he married her, and recorded it in Charleston. She was hot blooded and wolf clan too. Wanted her own ways."

"Johnboy was there - saw him do it Matt says."

"John Junior was no doubt right there in the middle of it. That boy tracks about in his troubles all the time - on the lookout for wrongness, he is - all the time."

David looks down, "Well... he's waiting for us now - back down there at that last crick bend, with the rest of the Euhaw." He takes a deep breath and blurts:

"The captain was hoping that some of these Cheraw could find us a shortcut to the Cape Fear or White Oak river - or maybe an easy portage over to the Neuse."

"No." Raymond says. "And I don't think that is even possible. But look here. You see those two fighters over there? They look like Westos to me. You can take them off my land when you leave - or better yet send them off with your Euhaw bucks, and you stay here with me. Forget all this dissension up the coast - it's a hornets' nest up there and you would do well to keep out of it."

"What's Westos, then? A tribe?"

Raymond stops and checks his thoughts. "A tribe? Yes David, a tribe. A most frightful tribe they were - at war with everyone - always on the hunt. The people said they were ashkanaza - cannibals - but that's not likely and I never saw any evidence of it. They hunted for slaves and booty though - like pirates - river pirates. They caught slaves and took 'em to James Town first - then later on moved down to Charles Town - always chasing their prey - chasing the people."

"Ye was a trader then?"

"I... I was one of the first actual Englishmen to arrive in Carolina, David - stepped off the boat in Charles Town on June

6, 1679 - tasked by my friend Lord Colleton to engage with the aborigines and discover any 'treasures that they might hold dear.' We were looking for gold of course, but not just gold - anything that was portable and worth the expense of shipping. So, yes I was a trader. The commission did not say so explicitly, and there was no licensure then anyway ,but that was it - trader."

"And my first task was to accompany John Wright out on his route. He introduced me to all the settlement Indians thereabouts then. They were the Kiawa - Cusabo - Sewee - Hopsewee ... I cannot recount them all now... but they all grew corn and lived in neat little round houses... and... and all the clans seemed to be happy and healthy, it looked like to me. All glad to be living near the settlers. They took a great liking to our trade goods, of course, literally cherishing all the metal - but what they cherished even more so was the security of living so close to the English. In short, we kept them safe from the Westos. That was the way of it then."

"Matt talked about some enemies one time - they took Yamassee for slaves - the Chichimeca?"

"That's them - Westos is what the English say. They were a folk unlike any I'd ever seen - not then anyway. They had no fields, no livestock - nothing. -- They lived almost their entire lives on the hunt, David! If it had hair or wore a skin they killed it. Excepting it was an Indian woman or child, mind you. Those they took alive and tied up in hemp rope - which they got from us."

"They traded those poor souls then for lead balls, knives and hatchets - and muskets of course. The other tribes called them Richachrician - Kanashashen - people eaters - but I never saw anything like that. They did eat a lot of smoked meat though. They had skins hanging everywhere David. All of them! Possums, raccoons, wolves, bear, beaver - and lots and lots of deer."

"Cougars?"

"No, but they had some other cats - lynxes and foxes. They lived as squalid a way as anything you can imagine, son. The stink and smoke of that place - God - it stunned me - to my very core. And I prayed most earnestly then - in my mind - through most of it. I stayed with them for two days and nights, that first time. -- John traded 10 muskets, a large quantity of lead balls, forty good knives and hatchets for the Indians they had taken - 2 women and 3 children. We took those poor souls and all of the deerskins there - 227 in total - and the beaver, I forget now how many - and some other skins too, of little value."

"John said that it was a slim return for the semester and doubted he'd profit any on the deal - but - if ye dicker with the Westos then 'ye'se apt to meet with yer maker Bray - and that right quick, eh.'" Raymond tries an attempt at Wright's accent, then goes on to say:

"I, of course, took no part in the negotiations then. Just learning my trade, as it were - and all of that time I was reconsidering my prospects here. Most fervently reconsidering - believe me." Raymond looks away for a minute - remembering. David starts to say something then stops - looks at Raymond for a bit - then figures a minute is plenty.

"So - the Westos, uncle - what happened?"

"That encounter with the Westos was... it was just a bracing, son - just a bracing. I kept my wits about me, kept my mouth shut for the most part, and took nary a scratch nor insult from any of that bunch. You hear me? They ignored me for the most part. So as fearsome as those Westos appeared to me - with all their wretchedness and all that damned smoke - it was only just a bracing for my first encounter with the Savannahs."

David pipes up, "Oh - the Savannahs? I've seen 'em - been past that village a couple times now."

"Village? -- Yes, they are 'settlement Indians' now I suppose, growing corn and peas - I reckon in rows now too, eh?" Raymond smirks here, and it makes David think of Pauline. "Well, when I first met them they were as strange to me as the Westos - horrifying to look upon - at first anyway. They were hunters and gatherers, like the Westos - and the best archers I'd ever seen. They had these medium curved bows with shafts made from the choke cherry tree here. You know it?"

David nods and asks, "How far?"

"How far what?"

"How far could they shoot?

Well - maybe 20 - 25 yards - that first time anyway... but they never missed a shot , David! Never! Even the young lads, they did not miss one shot. Not a one! You should have seen those people then David - the things they did." He looks down shaking his head.

"So what happened? Tell it man, do the telling - no matter how sordid."

Raymond draws a deep breath. "I came here in summer, and in the winter I saw to the destruction of the Westos - camp by camp. The Lord Proprietors afterwards saw fit to grant me 2500 acres for my services - to plot out wheresoever's I wanted here in this wilderness - and so ... now ... here we sit."

"Ye did not stay though - not then."

"No. I had firmly decided that the Carolinas were not for me and bought passage back to England. And after all I'd seen - well... I decided that business was not to my liking anymore and determined to read for the church. At Saint Mary's. " He takes another breath and goes on.

"My cousin and good friend Thomas Bray - your cousin too, David - we both took our orders together on December 5th, 1691. And all was well and good for us then - for a time. But through it all I had so many dreams about this place. Strange, fantastic things - of being caught up in tornadoes - and trapped in giant mounds - with bamboo trellises stretching up into the sky - with cougars chasing me and the people up and down the trellises - climbing and then dropping away to save our lives. All those memories - those visions - they never left my mind."

"Then one day - while I was living at Leeds - Thomas told me about a new mission objective - to establish schools and build libraries in the American wilderness, as a check to the spread of ignorance and dissent in the new world. Well... those words stuck with me David - stuck good."

"So I began to wonder about it in earnest then. About the spread and the depth of ignorance here in this new world." Raymond is animated again and nodding at David.

"I knew then what I had to do. I went to see my good friend Lord Colleton and told him it was high time I looked to my Carolina plat, and then I went to see the bishop. Two months after that I sailed into Charles Town harbor again. And this time... on my way back into the Indian Lands, I ... I found Donna - Pauline's mother." Raymond looks away for a second, remembering her. "We then built a home on that little bluff you saw back down there. I applied to the Society for any worthy, free printed materials that I could use to start a library - many times I wrote to them. And the next year they granted my request and sent me a good many books - numerous tracts - and 20 pounds sterling every year for three years after that. And with that money I was able to improve the grounds there and construct that little library you saw."

"I saw it."

"Well... after three years we were cut off from any support. The Society's Secretary wrote to me that the local Anglican Church members should provide for my needs. Hah! I had been there nearly four years by that time and had no church members to speak of, eh?" Raymond starts chuckling.

"Donna was Catholic. And we had debated our differences of

opinion on doctrine until I tired of it and let her be. Pauline was very little then."

"I...well... Donna. She learned we could get money from turpentine and other pine products - for the navy. So we got us another source of income for a while." Raymond is smiling and looking off again.

"We had a fine garden, David. Grew all sorts of things. Donna taught us, me and Pauline - how to trap fish and small game. So we never lacked due to her."

"And once a month or so we'd travel down to the lower towns, and then Donna would speak to the people. We'd exchange gifts - herbs and salves - medicines she'd made. But it was mostly just us - me and Donna and Pauline - them working the garden - doing their thing, keeping busy... and me."

"So when the Euhaws showed up across the creek it was like manna from heaven to me, son. Instant community! Hah! Mostly Catholics mind you - but also plenty of cheerful heathens, and just what I needed." He looks back at David.

"Those were the happiest days of my life right then, no doubt. And Pauline, she was the light of my eye. A joy to teach she was. I remember when she could first put "m" and "p" together, for jump - her smiling up at me. I knew she loved me then. The daughter I never had, David, but given to me nonetheless."

"What happened to the Westos? They sold other Indians for slaves right?"

Raymond scowls now, "Yes. Damn it all! That is the chief export in the Carolinas, as you know - second only to buckskins."

"That's the way folks make money here ye mean, deer skins and slaves."

"Beeves too. There's no end of cow pens around now. But beef money don't pay like buckskins, nor slaves... all ventures you'd do well to avoid here, David."

"So what happened to the Westos?" David is persistent if nothing else.

Raymond collects his thoughts again. "Well, how should I put it?" He shakes his head and sighs.

"It is not a story for church, David. Back when I was newly arrived here, we were completely surrounded by aborigines, much more so than even now. They did not speak English but most could converse some in a Creek patois - if you understand me." He takes a breath and remembers.

"Here was the reasoning of John Wright and the militia. If you want to prosper in trade with the Indians - then you need to have some Indians who actually produce goods worth trading for, eh? And the Westos had pretty much run them all off - except for the Cafetequichi. And them being Westos, well... the traders never really felt safe around them, eh?"

"So what happened?"

"It was along about that time that a new tribe came into the low country - from up north, like the Westos. John Wright made their acquaintance first. Promised them guns and knives and pots and pans, bolts of cloth in red and blue - beads and trinkets. And of course that was just what they wanted. Why they'd come to this land we now call Carolina."

"Who?"

"Who? They were the Savannah I was telling you about! And not the Savannah you saw." Raymond takes a long drink of cider.

"So how'd it go?" David asks, taking a drink too.

"It was John Wright and myself. And a Cusabo buck what was said to be good with sign. Hah! Well... they had been looking for us. Englishmen."

"They had two Micos there in the camp, and we gave them both a musket to start with. And 10 trade knives - and for their wives a sack full of cast pots and plates - and 10 spoons - and a couple bolts of red and blue cloth, eh? Enough to make many a fine blouse or shirt but, no." Raymond shakes head.

"No?" David asks.

"No. That cloth got turned into ribbons so fast you'd scarce credit it, son. Tied up in the womens hair and draped over them - the young ones a running about with ribbons a trailing out after them. Hah! It was something to see David. Something else."

"And the Savannah - all of them, had this awful urge to touch me too David - fingering my hair, grabbing at me. The little ones too, one or two a latching onto my boots, the little scamps! In your pockets quick too, eh?"

"Of course I dealt with them as gently as I could. They did not manage to topple me over anyway. " He chuckles some and looks at David.

"So... neither Wright nor me knows not word one of their speech, eh? But we are right in amongst them and they all want to grab on us, like I said. We're busy fending off the little ones, and I hear then all of a sudden the older Mico call out! And then he makes a long speech, on and on. Then when he is done the young ones all take off. And the womenfolk ease away after that too." He smirks and smiles at the same time.

"I found out later they were just trying out the new pots. And the young ones was sent to gather in herbs. But for a while there it was just us menfolk. They built up a big fire - and all of us gathered around in a circle - all linked up - shoulder to shoulder - arm in arm - entwined so to speak - me and Wright too."

"Then one old man starts a singing - and we're going round and round - a singing and a dancing - a call / response song that I can't make sense of now nor repeat - with a couple of fellers doing a lot of deep grunting too - like a bear sound almost - lots of bass, but the only real tenor was the old man, eh?

"So there I was. Scared out my wits, going round and round - like in a nightmare, eh? But this one big fighter, not the Mico. He's not quite as intimidating as the rest. He's not smiling at me - but the way he looks at me... I think I might just make it through this alive. So I keep my wits about me again and just go with the flow - dancing around to the songs - one after another."

"Y'all just danced round all night?"

"No. Not any part of the night in fact. It seemed endless then, to me - but looking back it was probably only an hour or two. The women had us something cooked to eat by then. A God awful mash of roots and seeds - and weeds looked like. Who knows what all was in that. Yech!" He shakes his head.

"If I never eat the like again, David, it will suit me well. But of course John and me, we both smiled and ate a proper amount. And the people kept on at us - touching our boots and feeling up our sleeves and coats - touching everything that we had - because it was all new to them see. Everyone there got a hold of me at least once I reckon." Raymond smirks and smiles again.

"So anyway, after we ate - I look over and see one of the young lads drawing back his bow and aiming it over at Wright's horse. Then I hear a man call out to the lad and he hesitates. Wright trots on over to him quick like then and asks the boy if he can try it - motioning to him - like he wants to shoot the bow. The lad, thank God, he understands and lets Wright have the bow. Then Wright hollers out to me.

"'Bray! Go fetch yer plate - quick - and hang it in the bushes yonder for a target.' -- Well fine I think, it's my own stock, but anyway - I go get it out my pack, hang it up in the bush and move away. John takes careful aim and bangs it dead center. Well that excites them up again and all the men go to grab their bows, and I don't know what to think now, eh?"

"But all they want is to shoot more arrows at that plate. I hang it up a couple of times, then one fellow comes up - motions to me and I let him take on that task. They kept on dinging away at that plate - one at a time - and not one miss - til the Mico calls out to stop. He had a few busted arrowheads, holding them in pieces there in his hands and that was enough. Then he talks a bit more to his men and gestures to one of the big fighters, who takes the plate and tries to bend it, but it is 1/16" steel with a ridge all around it so - hah! Then he tries to bite it, and everyone laughs at that."

"Then the Mico has him hang it up on the bushes again, and he goes off and brings back his musket. John loads it for him and he fires it off, and I see the plate go spinning up into the air. They run off and fetch it back and sure enough it's hit right on the rim - a big dent there but it's still a plate. So just as quick as they all got excited before, now they all got real quiet, and that was the scariest part for me, again. Then the young Mico starts calling out something - and he and some of the other bucks head off to the treeline. I figure they're out for a hunt and ask John and he says, 'What else?' Then the other Mico, the older one - he comes over, and signs for us to stay and sleep with them. So that's what we do."

"Then the next day when we get up John has a meeting with some warriors. Somehow he gets it across to them - that we want them to attack the Westos. And not just a raid - but to rub them out - kill all the warriors and take the rest captive. He told them that all the Savannah were to receive a musket each if they would help us."

"All of em got muskets?" David asks.

"Well..... No. We could only get 40 guns at that time - but it was sufficient. The next day the old Mico and some of his fighters just up and went to see the Westos - with John Wright and me along for an introduction. Wright tells the Westos that a large war party of Catawba are coming to wipe them out - and that the Carolina militia, along with our new allies here, the Savannah, would stay and join the fight with the Westos against our common foe. Together we can turn the Catawba's hunt into a hunt for the Catawba, eh? A proper ambush he said. And the Westos agreed. So.... a couple days later the Savannah fighters all make camp close up by the Westos. Me and John, we come up with the militia about midday and set up a camp. Then John goes out and makes jolly with them Westos all night - getting the fighters drunk on rum. They were all drinking and dancing; whooping it up way into the night. "

"So the next morning - it's bright and sunny early - the sky was a pale blue - the birds were quiet and it was just a bit of breeze. We walk up to that Westo camp - no lookouts since they're all sleepy from drink. -- The Savannah flank them left and right. Wright and me are in the middle with the militia, facing the camp. And then on a long whistle from Captain Moore we all give them a huzzah - until the fighters come stumbling out of their tents. Then the captain does his toot, toot whistle and calls out 'Fire!'

"And then we give them a volley. Boom Boom Boom Boom Boom - 70 guns at once. Then the Savannah start sending in the arrows - fast and sure, making every shot count. -- We reload in the middle and get another long whistle - the Savannah bucks clear back out and then on the call of 'Fire" we give them one more ragged ass little volley. Then all the Savannah run in fast with tomahawks swinging. The Westos are up now and swinging back, too fast to see - a dreadful furious thing that might have lasted two minutes altogether, eh? Then all the Westos are down - shot, or knocked in the head, and John Wright wades right in amongst the survivors, showing the Savannah, those still able, how to properly bind up the little ones what was left alive."

"Damn!" David cries out.

"Listen here David, and listen well. This is the part of the tale not made for the church. When I got back home I learned from Colleton that the Lords were very much displeased with the fact of the Westos demise, which they first learned about from me. And he cursed the men responsible for it - 'that bloody Barbados bunch', he called them. It turns out they killed all the Westos so as to get around Doctor Edward Woodward's one fifth share on the Indian trade. He was the proprietors man here and he made that original deal with them Westos. He was the first true Englishman to deal with the aborigines here. Englishman mind you - not Barbadian. There is a distinction." Raymond takes another deep breath.

"And so now with all the Westos gone, that Barbados bunch, all of them champing at the bit for slaves and booty, they took as their new trading partners the Creek and the Yamasee - like the ones you're traveling with now. You hear me, David?"

"Damn!" David says again. "So the Lords dinnae want the Westos done over, right? How come they give ye this grant?"

Raymond nods his head for a bit, then says.

"Because I told them the truth about it David. I went back with Dr. Woodward - back to England. I left voluntarily. But he was under a summons. The Grand Council here had denounced him, eh - to the Lords. Well, when we arrived back in England I assured the Lords that the good doctor had done nothing untoward the Westos, because I myself had seen to the end of all the Westos. You understand me. Not just that one ambush I told you about - but several. And then we had to track them and chase them all over God's creation. It took about a year, and when it was all done the Westos were extirpated - and the Savannahs severely reduced."

"So why did they give ye all this land again?" David asks.

"It was nothing to the Lords - the monies from the quitrents here, I mean. And they discovered through me that the Grand Council were their real enemies here, eh? The Lords wanted a fixed percentage of the trade - but that Barbados bunch got the Lords agent sent back in disgrace - the good Doctor Woodward.

I conversed the Atlantic with him and learned his story. And when the Lords brought him to court I testified that he had not seen to the Westos destruction - because I was there for all of it, and Woodward was not involved. It was James Moore, George Boone, Alfred English, Maurice Matthews, and John Wright to name a few. They were the primary actors. The militia men who started and conducted that war - most of them from Goose Creek."

David says, "Just north of Charleston, right?"

Raymond nods and says, "All those troubles up in North Carolina are likely to rebound back here son, and soon at that. I implore you, do not take up on this path. It is an Indian thing. Let them handle it. You stay here, and I can show you as fine a spot for a watermill as God ever made - waterfalls all around us."

David points over, "There's July." As he walks up with the cittern and banjo.

The mockingbird circles over a bonfire. Raymond has the cittern - standing with a strap over his shoulder - July is sitting on a log stool with the banjo on his knee.

Raymond calls, "All right now people - get ready to take a seat."

"Sit down on what? The dirt here?", asks David. And July replies, "No sir, just listen a bit."

July then starts the note part of the old spiritual "Why Don't You Sit Down" Raymond starts playing the rhythm - an instrumental beginning.

July: Why don't you sit down?

Raymond and chorus: Lord I cain't sit down.

July: Why don't you sit down?

Raymond and chorus: Lord I cain't sit down.

July: Why don't you sit down?

Raymond and chorus: Lord I cain't sit down - cause I just got to Heaven - got to look around.

Then a tinpan, rattle and a flute join in - along with some clap slapping and whistles - a short instrumental interlude.

July: Oh who's that yonder?

Chorus: Dressed in red

July: Must be the children

Chorus: That Moses led!

July: Oh who's that yonder?

Chorus: Dressed in white

July: Must be the children

Chorus: Of the Israelites

July: Oh won't you sit down?

Chorus: Lord I cain't sit down.

July: Oh won't you sit down?

Chorus: Lord I cain't sit down.

July: Oh won't you sit down?

Chorus: Lord I cain't sit down - cause I just got to Heaven - got to look around.

Lo--orrrd I just got to heaven - got to - look around.

At the end David calls out, "Whoooeee! What did ye call that thing - a Banjer?"

"Give it to him July - let the lad take a gander." He offers it and David takes it in wonderment . Plucks a few strings with his fingers.

"Did ye make this?"

July nods, "I copy it - ofrogee - from de Bantu. Before tonight I ain't never heard it right though - not like this. God bless you sir - these metal strings - they muy mojo - most righteous.

"When they start to turn - clean em with a bit o good whiskey. Real whiskey mind ye - nae rum!" -- Folks laugh and David hands the banjo back to July.

Raymond hands him the cittern, says "You play us one David, something from back home."

David hesitates, "No I ..."

"C'mon son - name it." Others say, "Sing us one David - play it - play one."

"Alright then, but be ye forewarned, it's an Irish tune."

They play again, Cittern and banjo - just David singing this time, a sad, but spirited lament about a mother looking for her soldier son to sail back home.

After the song is done one of the young ones, a little three year old girl, runs up and hugs David's leg - long black curly hair - brown eyes - and talking up a storm. She's looking up at David - arms wrapped around his leg. He's still holding the cittern and is a bit wobbly from drink. No one understands her.

July says, "Thas my sista's chile, poor ting. Sie Mae, she jest passed on - of malaria most like - may her soul rest in the Lord's keep." He looks at David.

"This chile - she ain't spoke nary a word since she been born sir. Not a word - not one that I heard- and I hain't no idea what she's sayin' to you now. None."

"Well - she's a pretty little thing, ain't she?"

"You take er then sir. We dont... I don't know what to do with the chile. The womens here, they don't want er. Say she wrong in the head - bad medicine."

David is more than a little drunk - shakes his head, "Wellll..." He's looking down at the little girl holding onto his leg - who's looking up and again saying something in earnest it appears. "I... I think I...."

CHAPTER 29

DAVID COMES BACK FROM THE WAR

Several months later - after the Tuscarora nation has been cut in half and subjugated, the Euhaw company finally makes it back to town - by boats, loaded down with plunder and captives, in the Big Spring of 1713.

David tells Pauline, "This girl here come from Raymond's, right? She ain't a capture. She don't talk to nobody but me - and I ain't got clue one as to what she's going on about when she does. But she minds good - fetches, and is real helpful like. I think she understands some English, but I ain't sure Pauline. Anyway, her ma has passed on and... well, I figured she could use some learning."

Pauline's eyes pop big - flabbergasted for once, she looks to the girl and back to him, asks "What then? Did you trade for her, David?"

"No, no. It's not like that. She's an orphan and er uncle just wants what's best for 'er, right? He's a friend now... and I just - I thought ye could maybe fix her - if she needs fixing that is." He's looking at most Pauline intently - hasn't seen her in almost a year now. "What d'ye think? I figured ye'd want 'er."

Pauline studies the girl for a bit. "I am happy to accept this challenge David - a blessing to us both, perhaps. She will be my daughter from now on; my first."

Then right after that Pauline grabs David by the arm and points at a young Tuscurora captive - about 9 years old.

"Get her too David - for us!"

David frowns, "She's Matt's."

"Mattias?" Pauline asks and David nods. "Never mind then", she says.

CHAPTER 30

DAVID GETS ANOTHER GIRL FOR PAULINE

David approaches Matt at the beach.

"What ye looking to get for that girl, Matt?"

"Saaay what? Now what would you be wanting with another little girl, brother?" He thinks a second then grins - knowing. "Ohhh, I see."

"I got 20 pounds Sterling coming to me in bounty. Ye can have all of that."

"What is Sterling to me man? I have made it so far alright without him."

"I'll give ye a pistol for her then."

Matt looks stunned - impressed for just a second, then frowns - shakes his head. "What good's a pistol to me man? Make it the long gun and it's a deal."

"That gun's no good for deer Matt - and ye took a musket this time right?"

"So what? I can get deer with my bow brother! And that musket - well you know. It's the long gun... or I see Pauline myself about the girl."

David says, "Deal." -- They shake hands.

CHAPTER 31

DAVID SAVES A MOCKINGBIRD

Pauline and David are out walking towards the creek. He says, "I have seen a strange thing of late."

"Tell me."

"Well... it started last week - the morning after I got back - settled and all. I was just coming out of the woods yonder, right - and I saw a little fox, a grey one, make a quick hop. And then it just sits there. Still like - tail pointed back and twitching - like a cat on a mouse. So I ease on over and she starts looking over at me and skips around a bit. Then I see this little grey bird there on the ground, right in front of her. The bird is so still... I thought it was dead at first - then it looks up at me. So I pick up a little dead branch and I whip it on the ground at the fox and she scampers off - but just a bit - I can still see her. I look down at the bird - and slide the branch up under im and he grabs on. Then I lifts im up a bit and he takes off - flying sideways like over into the next tree and hits it hard but still manages to catch on there anyway with his claws. He was about waist high up the trunk. And the fox - she's still hanging around - looking at me and the bird - back and forth, back and forth. "

"So I hold the branch out for a perch again to the little bird - and just as it touches im he flies away. Up and gone this time for good I thought."

"But - all this past week I keep seeing this little bird all over - flying in close and hopping around on the ground near me - not like other birds do, right? And she - or he - it's just looking at me - it's the same bird. I'm sure of it. Anyway... anytime I'm around the house now I see that little grey bird. And so just now before I saw ye - I was wondering where's the little bird right? And it dawned on me then that it was the same kind of bird what swooped on me when I first got here. I told ye about that, right? The one what knocked me out me perch, when I was up in the tree, and the big hog after me?"

Pauline is laughing, "I remember."

"So - just a bit ago - here comes the little bird swooping in again, and he lights up just on the trellis over there - not 10 foot from me. Then he starts in a singing his tunes - seven of em in a row. I counted - pretty, real pretty things!"

Pauline nods - recognizes the behavior and names the bird, "A Mockingbird! This is a good thing. It shows something about you David."

"How's that?"

"You will see - listen." She gives a whistle. -- "Was that one of its songs?"

David nods, "Yep." He starts trying to imitate Pauline's whistle.

"Do the rest of them", she says. He makes a few more attempts - then goes back to the first tune. He nods at her.

"Mockingbird, David, most definitely. If you were Euhaw that could be your new name - your warrior name. " She adds with a sardonic grin.

"But I'm not Euhaw."

"It matters not to the bird." She looks away - birds singing all around - turns and looks him in the eye and takes his hand. "We should get you cleaned up for the Busk."

"What is that exactly? And don't say you will see."

Pauline makes her demure smile. "The Busk is the green corn feast. A young corn that is perfect for roasting, with no soaking in lime, no curing, no mortar nor pestle. It is a simple feast - like the old times. Come on then, I'll get you fixed up proper." They keep walking towards the creek.

"Going to keep that beard?"

"I don't know." He rubs his short beard and looks at Pauline. She puts her hand out and touches it.

"Keep it for now - takes longer to grow than it does to cut."

They get to the creek and Pauline does not go in, but says, "Alright, let's have them clothes off, then."

"Everything?"

"Up to you David." He undresses. "Now take the rag and this soap here, and let us see what you can do, eh?" David goes in starts bathing.

"Lather it up good. Get that rag thick with foam, David." He washes all over and looks up at her when he's finished.

"Now, rinse the rag out. -- And again please ... come here now. Let me see."

He comes out. She takes the rag and soap and turns her attention to his ears and face, neck and chest and says, "Lift your arms up." Then she 's foaming up the underarms good.

"Go rinse off again."

When he comes out again she gives him oil for his hands, face and neck.

"This is palm oil David. Can you smell it? Very sweet, is it not? It does wonders for the skin too. It only lasts so long though." She massages it into his shoulders, face, and neck - sniffs and nods to him. "It will do."

CHAPTER 32

THE FEAST OF THE BUSK

David and Pauline arrive early and see the start of the Busk.

Pauline says, "First they dig the pit. You see the wood and charcoal there. They will spread that out and light it up in a bit. Then the men will walk on it some to stir it up; get the embers going."

"Walk on the coals!? Barefoot?"

"Not coals, not yet. But walking on them in just the right way gets it going quick, eh? It takes an hour or so to get the coals glowing just right. Then the women toss in the new corn, in the husk still - onto the coals. Then the men lay down palm fronds all over of it - so that just a wee bit of smoke comes out, eh? Makes for a nice slow cook. Muy bueno. The green corn is something else, David. Something new for your senses."

The people gather around the pit. The Mico calls out, in Muscogee and then the men come in and uncover the feast. Then the Mico starts talking again - quietly now, and all the people sit completely still. The sound of songbirds and running waters is all else that's faintly heard. Pauline does not translate word for word, but paraphrases very softly - close to David's ear.

"He reminds us that we are a white town, and that peace is our way. He says if you have wronged any one here, and have not made it right; then now is the time to ask for forgiveness. And those who have been wronged. Now is the time to forgive. And not a mockery of reckoning, with eyes and smiles, but a reckoning of the heart. This is the way of the people. We stand as one! All of us!"

The people shout then as one. They are a peaceful town and have already settled all their grievances earlier in the festival. If they had not, then nobody gets to eat - and they are close to starving now, having fasted for days.

They peel off the shucks. Very small ears are eaten almost whole - leaving just the nub - husks and cobs are tossed into the pit. It is a festival of satiation.

Around dusk the dances start - tin whistle, flute, rattles and drums.

Pauline asks, "Shall we have another go of it then, sir?"

"Yes mistress Bray. Yes indeed."

The Busk dancing is even more spirited than the Harvest dance - with the same evidence of pairs leaving - except this time David and Pauline leave together.

CHAPTER 33

THE STORY OF DONNA AND THE BEAVERS

Pauline and David are in her bed the next morning. She has her arm over his shoulder, nestled behind him under the blanket, both lying on their sides.

"Pauline - where's your mother?"

"She rests close by, love."

"Why'd they name you Pauline?"

She rises and leans over him, then gets up and gets dressed, as does David. He follows her outside to the little bamboo bower trellis filled with morning glories - with a bench now and they sit, the vines running overhead.

"She lies here, David." And Pauline waves her arm below the bench. "I have not spoken of her to you before, as it is not the way, but I do not think she would mind me telling you her story; not now."

"She was born into a people the Spanish called La Tama; far off in the lands west of here. The women there tended crops and raised children, as we do. And the men hunted then, same as now."

"When she was very young, a child no bigger than a beaver... her people were raided by Westos. Yet she managed to avoid capture by hiding herself with the beavers. She said that the pater and mater, both of them much larger than her; that they did not want her, but that both the pups loved her, so she was allowed to stay."

"She lived in the dam?

"Well... she gathered things on the land in the daytime, as she was taught, but at night she slept with the pups. -- Then one day, out on her gatherings, she came upon another group of Guale survivors, also on the run from the Westos. And she realized then that she was people, and not beaver. She went back to say goodbye to her friends, but they were not at the lodge."

"So then she left. And that was how she joined her first group of refugees. -- Those people, a mix of folks... pieces of clans. They all headed south. Seeking the protection of the Spanish. Once in Florida they stopped at a small mission."

"And there my mother grew up to be the town's greens woman, a healer, as you might say. She married there, and on the day after her wedding the Westos raided them again. Her bridegroom was killed in the attack, but she managed to escape capture once again, and soon led her own group of refugees. All headed even further south now, to another mission village called Ignatius, just five miles north of St. Augustine. And it was there David that she came to embrace the true faith, as she called it. She resumed her work as a healer, and became the concubine to the Alcalde there."

"Did she speak English?"

"Yes. She spoke many languages David. All the Muskogee dialects - and Spanish as well of course. Let me continue her story. So... all the missions of St. Augustine were attacked again in 1693, this time by the Yamassee. And my mother was caught and taken captive this time - bound in chains and taken up to Altamaha." Pauline lifts an eyebrow, and gives her sardonic smile.

"And there in Altamaha she was retained by an Anglican minister posted to the Indian Lands. He spoke some Spanish and quickly ascertained her native intelligence, and her value as a conduit for propagating the Gospel to the inhabitants of the Indian Lands, which was one of his mission directives. From Altamaha they traveled to this bluff here, and built a house of bamboo, with an oyster shell foundation and a planked cypress floor."

"When the Euhaw arrived across the creek there (nods) she again took up her work as a greens woman. And Raymond buys her a boat so that she can travel about on their ministry. And I went with her, sometimes. She taught English here first David, and the never ending count, eh?"

"When I was ten years old, Raymond signed papers emancipating her, and myself. And not a stipulation he said, even though I was not of age. I have them here still, and we have that boat too now David, still. -- She will always be with me, love. I am her only daughter. Her soul is twined in mine."

CHAPTER 34

AS TO HOW PAULINE FOUND MATTIAS

Pauline and David are at the trellis, having tea.

David says, "Matt tells me that you raised 'im - pretty much. I figured that was about ye teaching him English and all." Pauline takes a sip of tea and gives him her bemused look.

"So what happened to him?" he asks. "His folks get killed or something?"

"I did not teach Mattias English, David. I taught him Creek; taught him better English. But he had English in him when I found him."

"Found him? What do ye mean? Who lost him?"

Pauline smiles and says, "That is an interesting question David, and one I have managed to look away from so far."

"How old was he then - when ye found him?"

Pauline humphs and looks up to the sky - back to David, "God knows - maybe 10, or 11? His voice had not changed yet, yet he was taller than me even then."

"Where'd ye find him?"

"Hah! -- You and the questions this morning!"

"Just tell me where you found him, then."

"I found him on the Coosawatchie, just north of Tulafina. Had him a little islet all there to himself, did he not? He caught fish there I reckon, and had a mound of stones set close by for birds - or trouble maybe. I remember those stones; thought maybe his folk were buried there at the time, but looking back on it now, I doubt it."

"Why's that?"

"The people use stones like that to mark a passing sometimes, especially in the wild lands. That was my first really long paddle after Raymond left, David. I was curious as to how far the river went back then. Never been past Tulafina since."

"Anyway, as I was paddling back Mattias just ... popped up out of the grass! Said he saw me go by and when I came back, he couldn't help himself. He had on a moss weave cap, proper English shoes, breeches and a shirt. All very well made as it turned out. We copied the breeches, and even though the shirt was in tatters we managed to copy that too. Care for some more tea, love?"

CHAPTER 35

A TRADER GETS BANNED FROM EUHAW

Pauline assigns tasks to the little ones - finding things. So the new girls - little Gema, and now 10 year old Emma are soon out gathering herbs and berries in the woods nearby.

Pauline begins: "The story I heard, from Gemi, is that I banned all the traders from Euhaw. That I was a witch; had the evil eye, and now no white man dared cross my path. Hah! The truth is, that I talked to the Mico about one trader. McCray, who offered little else but lead balls and doctored down rum here, not fit for swill, much less for people to drink. I said it was poison and ought to be banned!" She shakes her head and looks down. "I was with the Mico when he told him to leave and never come back. Jeffery and Mattias were there too."

McCray is a trader in his 20's - as tall as Matt and big - weighing well over 200 pounds, bearded and blonde.

The Mico says, "McCray - I am sorry it is this way - but you are to leave the Indian Lands now. And not to come back - rum is outlaw - you are outlaw."

McCray answers, "But I have license to trade here, sir - and a large investment now too, right? I can get another post, leave ye be if that's what ye really want - but I have to have what's owed me first. If I don't pay me own debts, then what? The bankers sends the bailiffs out to me claim and takes it in arrears - and takes me off too if they can catch me. I'm going to have to have some kind of payment here, Johaniion - have to!"

Pauline interjects. "I have written to the Governor about you, sirrah, stating that you, William McCray have sold rum unto the Euhaw, on credit; and have threatened to enslave their wives and children for non-payment of these illegal debts! Rum is outlawed now in the Indian lands, in case you did not know. And all traders are forbidden now to sell anything on credit, anywhere in the Indian Lands. These acts are written down in Charleston, sirrah, drafted by your own assembly. You should go there and read them well. And know this. If this complaint were to go to a hearing, you would likely face a fine, and the forfeiture of your license to trade."

The Mico and several warriors are standing there - along with Matt and Jeff. All can see the hatred in McCray - powerless - and Pauline too. The warriors are standing stoic. The Mico looks a bit sorrowful.

Pauline remembers the scene and frowns. "The other traders stopped coming here then too, as a show of solidarity with McCray, I guess. Good riddance, I thought at the time. But looking back on it now I see it was not necessary for me to witness his banishment. The men could have taken care of it without me. It was him giving me the evil eye; so I should have known then what he was about."

CHAPTER 36

A GIANT TAKES AWAY GEMA

Emma comes back with a report that McCray has taken Gema.

"A giant - with hair like the sun!" -- The mockingbird sees it all, as it happened and just as Emma tells it. She's winded from running and starts in gasps.

"We were gathering - in the woods - she was not far - I could see her. And then we heard something - so we both dropped to the ground."

"Gema leans a little bit and the giant spots her. He looks around for a second and takes his rags out, one little one - one much longer - a scarf - looks around again. He crouches down low and sprints to little Gema, grabs her up, jabs one rag in her mouth before she can hardly squeak, then ties the scarf around her neck and over her mouth. Then he runs off with her held tight in his arms, wriggling about."

Emma follows for a bit. It's hard for her because McCray is moving so fast. Then she sees him stop, lay the girl down gently and says.

"Shooooo, shoooo easy now, girl, easy." Then he binds her hands and feet together, loosens her gag some and fusses with it a bit - making sure she can breathe alright. Then he slings her up over his shoulder and starts off again at a brisk trot - all the while trying to soothe her down.

"Shushushush now girl - easy now shush - be good now."

-

Pauline runs to her canoe with Emma trailing and finds David at the beach.

"McCray has taken Gema!"

"McCray?"

"A trader - one who thinks I've wronged him. He's taken Gema!"

"From where?"

"The woods, just over there," she points. "Not five minutes past."

David turns toward the woods - looks around - thinking, "If he's in a boat it'll be in a creek up on ReorSha - you can meander up or down in them marshes at high tide - all the way from here to Port Royal almost - but you got to come out somewhere, and that's at Bat creek I betcha."

Pauline nods, "Yes - we get there ahead of him and drift; make the circuit."

"I'll get me guns." He runs off.

"Be quick!"

Pauline turns one way, then another - and then runs after David. The gulls circle overhead, calling out - over and over - interested? They both come trotting back to the canoe, load the gear in quick and paddle off hard.

CHAPTER 37

PAULINE AND DAVID CATCH UP WITH THE GIANT

The gulls watch as Pauline and David search along the coast. They paddle easy now; riding the tide towards Bat creek, Mcray's likely exit route. On the second circle of the mouth of that creek, David spots a canoe coming. They start to move towards it, and as they get closer it is clearly McCray and Gema. David takes a pistol up in hand and Pauline paddles harder now. McCray does his best but the vector is lacking. There is no way he can make it past them to the bay. When Pauline and David are about 20 yards out from McCray's canoe, he grabs the girl with one hand and tosses her over the side, hardly missing a stroke, then paddles on by, turning to the bank for a few strokes before jinking back again to the bay, never looking behind.

The seagulls circle overhead; their cries mixing with Pauline's as she turns the boat. David leans out in the bow and scoops up a squawking Gema from the choppy waters, crying up a storm. -- McCray makes good his escape, as the Gulls circle up and up, making their own cries - again and again.

CHAPTER 38

ALL PAINTED UP FOR WAR

Pauline rides the waves up onto the beach at Pocotaligo and sees Gemi.

"Hola Gemi - Hola Polina" -- Both are smiling. They talk in Creek.

Gemi: So - are you staying over?

Pauline: No - the tide looks good for me to head back in about 2 hours.

Gemi: Those hours - they have taken such a hold on you. Have you forsaken the Up Towns now?

Pauline: No - I got my little girl to tend to now. Priorities change.

Gemi: Got two I heard. From your new man - the white one - turned out better than you figured, eh?

Pauline: Hah - one of the girls is a good help - the other is a challenge.

Gemi: The one that needs tending.

Pauline (nods): Yes. She only talks to David - if talking it is. I still do not know her tongue. Maybe it is just babble, an intention expressed in sound, but with no meaning at all, just affection. I wish you could hear her.

Gemi: Meaningless sounds - fraught with affection?

Pauline: Yes.

Gemi : Is any affection truly meaningless?

Gemi: I'd like you to walk with me dear - something you should see.

Pauline: What?

Gemi: It shan't take up even one of your precious hours - walk with me.

They head up to the bluff - look off to the north at midday - watching the men at the smoke lodge - hundreds of men just hanging out - talking in groups.

Pauline: Painted!! What are they painted for?

Gemi: What do you think?

Pauline: No! (in English).

Gemi: See the old Mico there? In the big chair? That's Emperor Brims. The Ochese Creek are here - in force - and the Appalachee. Brims says he speaks for 186 towns now - including the Yamasee. I cannot tell you of all the towns Paulina. Some I have never heard of - far to the west. And the traders will be here soon - any day now Pauline. They are most likely dead men, dear. -- You see all of those warriors there? Look good. They all owe more buckskins than they can count - all on "credit" (English). But I have taken your lessons on numbers to heart dear one, and applied them recently. The men of Pocotagliao now owe 40,206 buckskins. The 10 towns altogether owe much more than that. -- And the Creeks - their own debts are beyond my estimation - but it all comes to the same result. They don't have the skins - nor any bounties. The deer are all gone as you know. This is bad. If they could round up a thousand skins today I should be surprised. So those traders... they are all dead men when they get here Pauline. They've done the dances. I don't think Brims can talk them out of it.

Pauline: The Euhaw owe no skins.

Gemi: Yes, and I wish that were true here too but many, many micos are gathered here dear one - speakers from all the clans and all calling for the red way. -- But Brims wants peace, he says - that if the debts can be delayed, and paid out in other skins - not just deer, but beaver and raccoon, wolf - like the old days - and at a dressed price which is fixed, or a half-dressed price but still fixed; then we can continue to live in peace and keep the white ways. If not, then it is war.

Pauline: Gemi! This is bad news.

Gemi: The Cherokee are on their way I hear - and the Catwaba - all the tribes.

Pauline: All the tribes that took Neoheroaka? The same now plan to take the English?

Gemi: (Nods) They have made their dances Paulina - you see the paint.

Pauline: How many are here now?

Gemi: Hard to say... (smiles with an ironic head tilt) Want to see some more?

Pauline: More what?

Gemi: More warriors - at the Chunkey. Count them for yourself, eh?

They head towards the Chunkey, walking into a stiff breeze as the gulls are crying overhead. Before they get to the clearing Gemi turns to Pauline and starts to say something.

CHAPTER 39

A RECKONING OF ACCOUNTS

Back outside the parsonage Pauline is cooking along with David at the portico.

"Warriors owing money to the traders is a new thing David, and not good. Trading hides for rum; against the Law. Then giving them more rum on credit, again, against the Law, and while they are drunk, to be accounted for later... not good. So... this credit, it never leaves their minds now. So much so that they cannot tell sign even. -- Cannot do much of anything except drink the black tea and smoke the pipe around the lodge. And the more they smoke the more they talk. Talk about just killing all the traders. They owe more than they can ever hope to pay. And some traders have made threats here, David. That when they come back they shall seize our children in recompense. Well...." Pauline shakes her head and takes a few deep breaths to calm down. Then looks up.

"How can we make an accounting of this David?" She grabs a hold of Emma.

"How much is this girls life worth here? How much in pots and pans, or knives and plates; or pounds sterling?"

David is not wanting to say anything but, "Well I gave Matt me da's fowling piece for her - so 40 guineas at least - but that's four times what she'd a fetched in Charleston."

"What would that be in knives then - like you have?"

"Knives don't cost much - she's worth more than all I got."

"40 then?"

David shakes his head, "More - way more."

"What about buckskins then David?"

"I don't know Pauline. You can figure this stuff better than me."

"Make a guess!"

"Dressed?"

"Yes! Dressed buckskins."

"Two hundred then - maybe more."

Pauline shakes her head, "That's not far off David. A good guess."

"These beads here", she touches her necklace, "how many of these?"

"Well... I've been in the furnaces where they make em love - but I cannae give you a fair assessment of their value."

"An assessment now? Pray continue on then, David. Your guesses are improving the tone of our discourse. Hazard a guess please, the value of these beads here, in English pounds sterling?"

David is really not liking it now but is cornered. "A few shillings I guess."

"For each piece?"

"No, love - for all of em." He motions to the sides of his head with his fingers.

"Those beads - it's just glass. They're real pretty and all, but it's just glass - not jewels. They make em out of sand love, and sand don't cost nuttin."

Pauline looks horrified - she takes off a strand.

"So these beads here, they are made in the place you have likened unto hell?"

She takes the necklace to the table - inspecting it close and then taps it with the handle of her knife - then smashes her knife handle onto the beads, sending out a few glass chips.

David interferes "No, No!", and grabs her arm with the knife handle - gets kneed in the nuts and falls over still holding her knife hand. When they hit the ground she wrests it free and bounds up over him.

"What ails you sir!? What madness is this? To grab at me with a knife in my hands? If that's all you're good for then you should just get on somewhere. Get ye to your Uncle, sir. Or to the devil!"

Then she turns and leaves, running to the beach, and there takes the beads out of her hair, carefully, and casts them into the waters. She keeps one necklace though. Later on she comes back and David is tending to the cooking now.

David is stirring in the pot, and not looking up says, "If I leave here - without ye that is... then I'm headed back to Scotland - not to Raymond's. Me brother's still a laird there, ye know. I can camp on his land as well as here."

"Stay here then. Not safe for you to travel anyway."

David keeps stirring in the pot.

Pauline is teasing now, not mad, "If Emma was worth only a 10 guinea piece and your fowler worth more than 40 - pray tell then, dear one, why didst thou ever makest such a trade?" She likes poking fun of Quaker speech - even though she's never actually met one.

"Thou knowest very well why." David answers. "And I know what English debts do to people love. I've been to the poorhouse - and the castles."

"Whose castle?"

"Well... my grandfather's for one - Baron Grey of Ruthin. Me uncle Henry's the heir there, right - got lands in both Scotland

and Wales."

"Me da married Henry's sister see, and they all got on good together. And they played music - that's me earliest memories. -- But me da... he died when I was just a wee bit. I don't really remember much about im - besides seeing him and Uncle play. I saw im on a horse once - a big black'un." He shakes his head. "They say I look like im, but I don't remember im much. Sometimes now I dream about im though - that I'm riding that horse with im - hanging onto his back hard as I can - cause I'm still just a wee lad, in the dream, and we're riding fast across a red sea - filled with bones - blood and bones we're flying over - blue skies up above. -- These are the dreams I have now - since I got back, love. Before I came here - I hain't never seen a man killed before. Never, Pauline - ceptin at a hanging."

"Do not fret it, dear one. The past only catches up to us in our dreams. Here, let me finish this. You go start us some tea."

CHAPTER 40

INDIAN AGENT NAIRNE FOREWARNS THE GOVERNOR

The mockingbird flies over Agent Nairne and trader McCray on horseback, trotting briskly along Charleston streets. They turn and halt outside a gabled two story house. They dismount and hand their horses over to a liveryman, who takes them off, shaking his head at their frothy muzzles and wet coats.

The Governor comes out the front door.

"Nairne? What the devil are you doing back here, man? Has Wright brought yet another suit against ye?"

Nairne starts, "No ... well ... yes he did. Two more in fact - but that's not why I've returned. It's bad news, Charles - the worst. The Yamasee and the Creeks and the Appalachee ... they are all gathering in Pocotaligo."

"It's the debts, see. The Yamassee can't pay this year and some blasted trader to the Creeks has killed Brims little prince. So now they've all come to Pocotaligo - with Brims. And he proposes that you sir, should meet with the Micos - and arrange for new terms. They want more time to pay - they want the traders to take other skins besides deer - and they want to wipe away any rum debts accumulated. And they want fixed trade rates too - in writing. Brims has offered these terms and if we can make a deal then it's peace. If not - they are ready for war. Tell him McCray."

"I hain't never seen so many bucks in one place milord - lots of bigwigs too - hundreds and hundreds of fighters - Creeks, Apalachee, Savannah - and more the likes of which I hain't never seen before."

The Governor goggles at him. "How many?", he asks.

"I don't know, milord - more 'an I could count - might a been a thousand."

"Good God."

"Brims is said to carry a stick with 186 ribbons", Nairne tells him, "one for each town that has thrown in with him. And there's more on the way, Charles."

The governor is taken aback by the news - and sends Nairne and McCray, who might not be the best pick - back into the Indian Lands.

"You will ride out again today. You go back to Pocotaligo and tell the Micos that I will meet with them in Savanno town. Tell them that I come with shot and gifts - that we will smoke the pipe and listen well to all their complaints. I will send for the horse guard to assemble immediately, and meet you there."

Nairne says, "That will take quite some time Charles."

"Yes, but you will go now and have them remove this dispute to the Savannahs - and perhaps leave some of those warriors behind you in Pocotaligo, eh? Give me a week, Thomas - one week! Placate them - do whatever is needful. Take whatever stores and gifts you think fit and bill the assembly. Just hold them off, man! Hold them off!"

Shall not all these take up a parable against him, and a taunting proverb against him and say, Woe to him that increaseth that which is not his? How long? And to him that ladeth himself with thick clay!

Shall they not rise up suddenly that shall bite thee, and awake that shall vex thee, and thou shalt be for booties unto them?

-- The Book of Habakkuk - KJV 2: 6-7

CHAPTER 41

A VERY BAD GOOD FRIDAY -- APRIL 15, 1715

Both McCray and Nairne die on the Good Friday before Easter, in the Year of Our Lord, 1715, on the morning after their arrival in Pocotaligo.

Nairne is outside and sees the warriors coming for him, but he doesn't shout, doesn't go for his pistol. He knows very well what is about to happen and stays calm - ready to show brave. He's lived amongst the Yamasee - traveled with them all the way to the Mississippi and back - across the whole of the Muscogean lands. So he knows what's what, and keeps his cool.

McCray is attacked inside and shoots one warrior dead. He had his pistol loaded and ready - slept with it close. He roars up and stabs another fighter into the neck and batters several others to the ground. They tumble the little house down from the inside, fighting inside of it. McCray gets up from the busted bamboo and starts running, but only makes it about 20 yards. Just as he reaches the Chunkey field, a warrior throws a tomahawk, hits him behind the knee and he drops. Seven more men are there in a second and McCray is hit with so many tomahawk strikes it's hard to count. The others lead Nairne away and tie him up to the pole. First they will cut away his clothes with their knives. Later on they will stab his arms and legs with large wooden splinters, wetted with pitch, and then they will set him on fire.

CHAPTER 42

DERECHO MALO - BAD THUNDERSTORM

Matt is hollering and running up from the beach.

"Pauline! Pauline! Come quick!"

She meets him near the trellis garden - David is trotting up from the woods and fixing his belt.

"They've killed Nairne - all the traders too!"

"Where?" she asks.

"In Pocotaglio, and Huspaw. All the up towns. It's started. Jeff's gone to Chechesee to tell em it's time. My part is to get JoHannian and the Euhaw - tell em it's Big Spring."

"No! You will not!" Pauline stares him in the eye.

"Pauline - this is happening now! Right now! The Euhaw, the Okatee, the Chechesee and all the fighters from Altamaha are to gather up below Port Royal - and wipe it away with the next tide."

Pauline looks at Matt and then David - back and forth - thinks hard for a few seconds and shakes her head. "No, no, no. They will keep some traders to torture and set fire to first, eh? It gives us some time." She's nodding now and smiling grimly; says, "You and David will go now and sound the Alarum cannon."

David and Matt explode, almost in unison, "WHAT - In Altamaha!!??"

"Yes. They will be busy for a bit, having their last smokes, so to speak." She looks off - remembering.

"The fighters will not see you if you stay down low. The

chunkey is on the far side of the bluff from where that cannon sits. If you stay well below the chassis, they will not see you."

"The chassis?", Matt asks.

"The wheel frame," David says, then adds, "That powder's been sitting there for 10 years, Pauline."

"Take what powder we have then. And blow the bloody thing up if you can, David! But Go! Go Now!"

"I'm gettin me pistols!", he says and runs off.

"Get the powder!" She looks around." Mattias, I can inform the Mico of our situation. You wait here." She takes off running to the parsonage after David.

CHAPTER 43

ONE BIG LOUD BOOM

David and Matt paddle up to Altamaha and land at the beach. Matt says:

"We ain't got to creep on em, man. They's all at the cheney. Let's just walk on up there like we's supposed to be here." David nods and this they do - walking up to the bluff, seeing no one. They stop first to check out the little powder doghouse by the cannon - pull the front off and drag the barrel out and open it. It is nearly full of dry black powder.

"This powder here's good.", David says.

"Let's mix it up some with what we got just to be sure."

"Right."

They pour more than 20 pounds of powder into the cannon - pack it in with a rammer and then jam a wood block into the mouth - then light it with a long fuse of cotton streaked in turpentine and run away. -- BOOOOM!

The cannon explodes into pieces, with shrapnel shooting past Matt and David and as far away as the chunkey field. The shock wave catches them as they're running away and knocks them down.

They get back up - make it to the beach and start off in the canoe. Two Yamasee warriors run up - the drummers. They're painted in red and black, and both know David and Matt. The drummers stop at the beach - fire their muskets and one hits David in the back of the neck as he is paddling away. He's knocked forward, then jerks back to try and right himself and so collapses backwards into the boat. Matt paddles on hard.

The Yamasee reach their canoe and start after them. David twists around to press back up - stops to look at Matt, and spits a lead ball out of his mouth that makes a plonking sound on the boat bottom. Then he rights himself and grabs the paddle - coughs and spits some blood into the water - looks back and just before he dips it in he puts the paddle down and waves his fingers back to the pursuit - "Go back to 'em Matt - back", softly he says as he can't catch a good breath. Then he pulls out his pistols while Matt turns the boat around and goes with the tide - faster now. The Yamasee approach and David shoots them one - two - in passing. -- Then he takes his shirt off and binds it around his neck, grabs the paddle as they turn the boat around - once again against the tide.

CHAPTER 44

YOU ARE GOING TO LIVE

David and Matt arrive in Euhaw, where David falls out into Pauline's arms - who sits him down on the beach. She unwinds the shirt and scowls.

"What the? Gema! Fetch my bag! -- Emma! Get some water boiling and then get plenty of garlic. Be quick!" She turns, nice voice now, "David, dearest one - can you stand up?"

He nods and gets up - the wound in his neck starts bleeding again. She puts her kerchief on it and holds it there.

"Let's walk on up to the house now, shall we? Nice and slow David. That's right, love. Keep your neck still. I may have to wrap it again, but... if we take it nice and slow... there is no need. Listen to me now, dearest. You are going to live. It is already starting to knit. And it looks to me like the ball passed through. Into your mouth maybe?"

"I saw him spit it out - the ball, I mean", Matt says.

"Well, well... so it's a through and through then. Thank God! These are not difficult to treat. No problema, eh? You are going to live! Let us just keep easing along, as we do all the time. No hurries, and no worries at all us, eh? Living in Paradise. Don't say anything now, but stop here for a second and let me take a look at your spit, eh? Just drop what you got in your mouth, no straining now. Yes, right here." He spits on a stretch of sand.

"Hah! Hardly any blood at all. You are going to live, sir! No doubt in my mind! -- Let's keep on going slow now anyways - and keep your head still, eh? You are doing beautifully love. Just keep on taking it easy. " All of this with Pauline's purest most appealing voice - her welding voice.

They make it to the house and the girls open the door and they go inside. Matt waits by the porch. -- Later on Pauline comes back out.

"I heard the cannon, but I doubt Port Royal can know for sure what has happened - much less the rest of the province. Can you ....?"

Matt looks down, slowly shaking his head.

"No - I need to leave with this here tide Pauline. Take as much food with me as I can, much as you can spare I mean - and go. You... I will love forever - even if I don't never see you again. You know that. But they's no place left for me here now. Have you got some pemmican?"

"No. Got some fried cornbread though . And take one of those rabbits hanging over there if you want. Take both. Do you have a poultice kit?"

"Not on me - no."

"Wait here then. Let me fix you a package."

She goes inside again - in a bit she comes back out with some things.

"I'm headed to Florida, Pauline. They's a black town down there I'd like to see again. And if your lessons in Spanish prove sufficient, I may get to see the Governor, eh?" He smiles and looks sad.

"Jeff knows the way. He can find me there, or anywhere in the Floridas most like. If you see him tell him that." He reaches for her hand. "If for any reason... if you need me to come back here for you - or - if you just want to write to me sometime. Send a letter - por Mattias el Veritos - to the Spanish Governor in Santa Augustino - en Ingles. -- Correcto, si?"

"Si, correcto."

CHAPTER 45

A TIME FOR DESPERATE MEASURES

The Assembly hall in Charleston is packed with men. The governor is at the podium and looking out. -- The sergeant at arms pounds his gavel like a drum.

"All right let's have some order now!" The men are all engrossed in their stories - resulting in a din that dies down slow. There is a lot of shuffling as they settle down and the Governor starts.

"I have come to plead with you today, sirs - and pray that you make haste in your deliberations here. -- As you all know by now, the people have been put to flight - forsaking holdings, crops, livestock, everything. The missing and the dead number over 500 souls now - and it'd be a lot more than that if Port Royal had not heeded the alarum and taken refuge on board the Catalina - lying at anchor there. Let us all thank God for that. That with the arms of the people gathered aboard - and the little cannons strung along its portside, they were able to turn back a horde of over 400 Indians - with no casualties on our part. None!"

"Now... as to our response to these most heinous acts", he looks at his notes "we have... we have now constructed a total of 19 pallisades - from Port Royal to the south and up the coast as far as Winyah - all now full of refugees - starving inside of their cramped confines - sweltering and terrified - with malaria and yellow fever rampant. So we shall have more deaths to count soon enough."

"At least 90 of our 100 licensed Indian traders have been killed. That's right - the only ones spared were those absent from their posts. So... we're not going to have any income from the Indian trade - none. And since the people are all confined to the forts, we're not going to have much income at all - not from rice, indigo, nor tobacco. And the beef? Well, the beeves are all gone, sirs."

"So! We are in dire straits. Very dire straits indeed. With nothing but hard times to look forward to no matter what we do here. -- Such extraordinary times will require like measures from this Assembly now - as you are the only recompense to our emergency. Gentlemen... We have no Guineas to pay our militia - none to purchase supplies - and none for armaments. -- I propose that we immediately issue one million pounds of current paper credits - to purchase supplies for the war effort. -- And every man between the ages of 16 and 40 must be armed - and every male bonded servant that is deemed trustworthy should get a musket too. Indeed, all eligible men hereabouts should be enrolled in the militia - whether he be freeman, a bonded man, or indentured servant. "

"I adjure you - and plead with you - make haste now! Our very survival depends upon your swift concurrence."

CHAPTER 46

THE BURNING OF EUHAW

Early morning, as the fog lifts slowly from the waters - Pauline sees Jeffery rowing hard with another warrior as they come to the bank.

"The Governor's took the fort - and Captain Chicken has orders to wipe away all the towns now - burning houses - taking captures - all the people run. You go now - with us - Paulina!"

"Chicken must know that the Euhaw have taken no part in this. You can tell him that Jeffery."

"No - Kiawah and Cusabo scouts are here now - all the towns are to burn - wipe away. -- No more talk. -- Can David go?"

"David is not going anywhere - not today. When will they get here?"

"Soon - we must go now - you come with us. This place is no safe - no more! Paulina - please!"

"I cannot - cannot." She chokes up and looks across the creek. Some of the people are carrying their pots and pans and other goods - canoes are filling up.

Pauline is on the far side of the creek when the militia approach Euhaw. Whites and Blacks, an equal mix - and several Indian scouts. -- Some women and children are taken, and the plundering starts. One house is lit - then the rest. Pauline paddles across. She is shouting.

"The Euhaw did not attack you - they have lived by the treaty and are to be left alone. Any man who does harm here will answer to the Government."

A couple of white militia and two black men turn to her and one says "I reckon Nairne ain't taking no complaints now, missy. " Another fellow laughs. Then the reckoner makes a grab for Pauline.

"Keep your filthy hands off me!" She backs off - slapping hard. "By God you will rue your misdeeds here. __ These people are Christians - and you - a lot of witless curs. How did you even manage to find this place? Where is Captain Chicken?" Three men are checked by her eloquence but one says, "Lawdy, have ye ever heard such from an Injun - this'un here's mine boys and I aim to keep 'er". He grabs at her again and starts to bind her and she wails, "David, David Kilbernie!" And then kicks him in the nuts, bounces the gunbarrel off his head, breaks free, and runs away fast - where she's soon met by Captain Chicken, on horseback, who stops everything.

"Captain - these men have attacked me for no reason - chased me like prey - and David Kilbernie lies yonder - shot through the neck after risking his life to fire the alarum cannon in Altamaha - at my urging - and now with him lying on death's door, these filthy curs lay hands on me. I am sorry of..."

"Hold on there now, mistress - I know who ye be - ye're Daveys' Pauline as shore as I'm sitting on this here horse." The horse sort of buckles forward in a bow as Chicken leans in and tilts his hat.

"We're sorry to have troubled ye mistress - and I shore hope to hear soon of your bonnie lads speedy recovery. -- Best get on back to him now."

Whereupon the soldiers and Chicken depart - leaving her behind as they continue on, headed to the next town.

The Euhaws were the only Yamasee town not to kill it's traders, as none were present. And they did not send any warriors out to attack Port Royal. They were the confederacies newest white town. Jeff and all of the fighters - most of the people there, have slipped away. A few women and children are taken captive - the ones that did not leave the village.

Later Pauline finds David sitting at the portico with a pistol in his hand and a musket propped up next to him.

"I heard you calling me in a dream from way far away - and then I was awake. And then I heard you laying it on to somebody out there. I got the guns loaded, but I couldn't cross the creek. Sounded like ye had it sorted anyway. -- Was Chicken there?"

"Yes David, I took care of it. Chicken was there and they've burnt the town - what was left of it. His men tried to take me too but the Captain intervened and rebuked his men for the insult. -- One man tried to tie me. He put his hands on me." She's shaking her head - mad.

"David. Him you must deal with properly. Later - when you are better."

"I'm better now - hungry too. -- Did ye get his name?"

"I heard no names. And the Captain... did not take the time to make any introductions."

"What's he look like then?"

Pauline is almost overcome with anger again and says sharply, "Never mind!" She turns back around and walks over to the bank - as the widows come out from the woods. Pauline is looking at an empty village now - a desolation - track marks in the sand and embers dying away - no people.

CHAPTER 47

A NATURAL OCCURRENCE

Pauline wakes up with morning sickness. The widows take note and nod to one another, then continue on with their work. -- David is just coming out of the woods. He sees her and slips away - back into the woods. He hopes that this will perk her spirits up some, but he knows when to make himself scarce too, and figures now's as good a time as any to check some fish traps.

CHAPTER 48

DAVID MEETS THE GOVERNOR AND GETS A LAND GRANT

The Governor approaches the parsonage on horseback and calls out.

"Hallo there! Be ye David Kilbernie?"

"That'd be me," David hollers back, "And yer name, sir?"

"I am Charles Craven - deputized as Governor of this Province, and I have traveled here at the request of your elected Assembly to offer you their thanks sir, for your heroic and timely warning this Good Friday past. It seems our former allies the Yamasee, with the Creeks, the Apalachee - and now even the Catawba - all the tribes closest to us - those we counted on as our friends and protectors - they have all turned on us, and had likely wiped us out had you not taken smart action, sir. So - again - you have my thanks, the thanks of the assembly, and I daresay the admiration of every soul here what knows your name. I've come to tell you that the assembly has acted for you to receive a land grant of 690 acres, in the locale of your choosing. They would have made it more, but anything over 700 acres must meet with the approval of the Lords, and that can take a year or more, what with the crossing and all. So! Have ye any notion where ye'd like to settle, sir?"

"I do. There's a spot above my Uncle Raymond's claim that suits me well, very well indeed. I thank ye, sir. -- When can I be presented with the deed?"

"Come to Charleston with me now if you like - or as soon as you're able. -- You'll have to sign for the plat and register the deed there."

David nods at this, "'I'd heard ye took the Yamasee fort - up past Tomotly."

"Yes - a bloody mess that was too. We were fortunate they had not finished building it, otherwise we'd have been even more sorely repulsed. As it was they gave us several disciplined volleys. On our first charge we failed badly - turned tail and ran. Then Burroughs led them in again with fascines up front. The Yamasee kept up the fire but the balls were all spent in the brambles. We were right in on them and took the gate. Then... well they all took to the woods. I lost twelve men, many more were wounded, and we took just six scalps. So... they are still out there. The ten towns are destroyed - but all of their fighters are still out there. And the fields here are ripe with corn I see.

"Did they kill all the traders?"

"No they did not. Five licensed traders are alive still. At least that - the five that applied for the Poor Relief."

"Whooeeee! Traders living on the dole!"

The Governor laughs, "No! They are not Fund members - rest assured. I have seen them all now well employed in the militia, or the scoutboats - taking the scrip like every able bodied man here aught."

"I don't care for no more scrip, sir - not for no bounties, no how."

"Well... I have recently been assured by my agent to the Cherokee that they did not send any fighters against us, or that's what the Micos say. -- They are all very keen now to raid the Creek it seems - wanting our muskets first of course. We can trade with them again soon I expect. Major Moore says that they want everything else we have too - not just kitchen wares, but plows and farrows. They want the knowledge see - metalworking and such. And I'm all for it - whatever it takes to keep the peace with the Cherokee. You know what I mean."

"I do, sir. I was at Neoheroaka."

"Well, in any event, the Cherokee refuse to make war on the Yamasee - and we don't care about that. They're gone - back to Florida - or to the wilderness - who knows? But they are not anywhere in the Indian lands."

"Someone's working the corn here still. I know that much."

The Governor frowns and takes a serious tone. "Mr. Kilbernie - I recommend that you leave this place as soon as you are able - and take refuge in one of the palisades by Port Royal - either Blackwell or Wright's plantation is closest. Or... you are more than welcome at my own home in Charleston. Captain Burroughs there is at your disposal - if you should choose to leave with us now."

David thinks a few seconds - looks to the creek and the big piraguas. "I should like to see to my land grant immediately, then sir - load up and sail for the Seraw country - or as far as those boats there'll take me."

"I fear that the troubles here, though somewhat abated now, that they still require our scouting boats to remain here - in local waters."

"I heard the Catawbas hit the settlers hard - up around Winyah - but Chicken sent 'em running. He didn't take any towns though, did he?"

"No. That is the gist of it. The Catawba still have the north country - up to the Cape Fear river."

"Why not let me try for a new agreement with 'em then, sir - them and the Waccamaw - and the Wateree. It stands to reason. They remember me... and ... Pauline... Pauline speaks that tongue well enough. They all know of her too, sir - and would listen well to what she had to say."

"And what would she say?"

"Damned if I know sir, and that's the truth. She says what she likes." He chuckles, but then frowns and looks to the Governor, very serious again.

"I can ask her to try and make a peace for us - and she'd want that, I think. I'm sure of it. I know she wants those Euhaw what was seized over there". David points across the creek. "All of them women and children. If ye can get them back here - the men here would return and keep the peace, I believe, sir. They took no part in the raiding. And I think they're still around, somewhere - out in the woods. I hain't seen em but somebody here's taking in some corn."

The Governor sighs and looks down, "Those folk are all likely sold by now Mister Kilbernie. Regrettable - but nothing I can do about it." The Governor takes another sigh - and a deep breath.

"Captain Chicken sent me an account of their capture, but I have spent almost every day on horseback since all this started."

"How did ye know I lit the alarum, then?"

"I heard that from John Wright - that you saved Port Royal - kept it from being another Stuarts Town. He was the one who proposed to the assembly that they award you your grant, sir."

David considers this - shakes his head and says, "Well, I still want to leave and see to my land, Governor - and I need yon piraguas to take me there. Listen well here sir, an embassy of this kind is just exactly what ye need right now - to secure the north as quick as possible, before they decide to paint up again. We don't want that, do we? We can save a lot of lives - on both sides. And Pauline... she can be your ambassador to the Catawba - and them piraguas there with them swinging flechette guns should be enough to ward off any raiders we'd see. I'd want to take 40 muskets too - loaded."

"40 guns? The boats'll only hold 12 men."

"More than that I hope. We'll need some canoes then too.

And as many men as ye spare. I hope we won't need them muskets, but we'll have all 'em loaded and ready, sir. Cause when shit happens, it happens fast. We can give some to the Micos along the way, too."

The Governor thinks a few seconds. "When can you be ready?"

"Tomorrow - the tide rolls out before midday."

"You'll need to go to Charleston first and get your papers."

"We'll be headed there first then."

"Very well - I shall start back immediately - and give Captain Burroughs his orders. Godspeed to you David - and God bless."

The Governor goes towards the beach. David heads up to the parsonage and sees Pauline, says, "I reckon we need to get married, Pauline."

"In Charleston I suppose?"

David nods, "Where ever ye want, love. And we need to start packing."

CHAPTER 49

A FOULNESS IN THE AIR

When Pauline arrives in Charleston, for the first time, she gets sick again - chokes and gags coming out of the docks.

"Ohhh! -- This town. God save me! The smell. David! Are your senses not astonished? How can they live in such filth?"

David is non-plussed, keeps on walking. Then they see a woman walking out of a house with a pisspot in hand - slinging it wide. She grins at David - then returns waggling back to the house.

"Saucy thing." Pauline says and looks at David. "This place is awash in its own waste. I could never have imagined such." She holds a kerchief up to her face.

"It is a wee bit dank right here love - but nothing like back home." David notes a man with a fine suit walking their way and leads them on.

"Good day to ye, sir. I am David Kilbernie - recently arrived here. Do ye have knowledge of the slave market? Any recent or upcoming auctions?"

"Good day to you, sir. I am Clayton Grainger, esquire. And my office is just up the street there, and, yes I am familiar with the affairs of the market. I have handled many assignations there, many indeed."

"Have there been any auctions for Indians here - recently?"

"Why, yes. Just a few weeks past in fact - and it was the first such offering here in over two years - first since the Tuscarora troubles. They were Yamasee captures. Women and children, all sold now and departed, I'm sure."

Pauline cries out, "But the Euhaw did not take any part in the raids! They were Christians. -- Oh God! -- My people! -- What have I done?"

"And how do you know this ma'am?" The lawyer thinks they're married.

"How do you think sir? I saw it with my own eyes. Did I not have to fend off capture and run for my own life, as well?!" She shakes her head and the bitterness pours out. "All for this... this foulness flowing here. Well... I repent of it now. God forgive me!"

Here David tries to gently lead Pauline away, but the lawyer, who is genuinely shocked pleads with her.

"Forgive me then ma'am please, for I most surely did not wish to offend thee. I am indeed sorry to hear of your loss. And for all of our losses of late. I had never imagined such a thing possible - not before this Easter past. It is a hard living we have here now, compared to what we had. Good day to you." He nods and tips his hat - walks on.

"Let us go see the Governor, love. He's sure to know more about this." David takes her hand and says, "Don't lose hope. Not yet. Remember how we took Gema back from the maw, right - saved her from the underworld?"

Pauline looks up and decides to keep going - what else? But not talking - she is inside of herself now, resigned to more bad news.

CHAPTER 50

PAULINE MEETS THE GOVERNOR

They arrive at the governor's house. David and Pauline are quickly led into the study by the housekeeper.

The Governor is at his desk and rises when they enter.

"Good and well met sir! And it is such a pleasure to finally meet you as well, Mistress Bray. I have heard so much about you. All to your credit, of course. I am much indebted unto you, mistress, very much indeed." Pauline says nothing, but nods.

The Governor looks to David, "Are you well provisioned then? Ready to depart? I have given Burroughs the purse for this mission - but here in Charleston I should not want you to lack for anything that might advantage you - should you need something special to please one of the Micos?" He looks to Pauline and then back to David - pulls out from a drawer some cash. "Here are bonds I have set aside for such special provisions. -- I thought 100 pounds should prove sufficient for you."

David nods and says, "Well ... sir... we had not started on that really - I mean the provisions and all. We took all what we could fit on the boat here anyway. And I thank ye again sir, for all of that - but what we need now is help with something else - two things actually.

"What? -- Tell me now and if it is within my power it shall be done."

"A provisional promise sir?" David looks at Pauline, who frowns just a bit with a brief headshake. Then David says, "We want to get married."

"What? -- Married to whom?"

"To each other, sir."

"Well", the Governor shakes his head now. "How could I help with that?"

"Pauline here is raised Anglican - like yerself, sir - and she wants a Church Wedding. --- We have been... unable to make any announcements until now - us not living in Charles Town and all - ye see what I mean, sir?"

The Governor looks from Pauline to David and nods, "You said two things - what is the other?"

"Are there any people of the Euhaw - the Yamasee - any left here in Charles Town?"

The Governor thinks a bit then says, "As it happens - there are several young girls staying now in the Parson's stables - quarantined there for smallpox. Although I heard they all survived and are in good health. And it appears they all speak English, to the astonishment of the matrons. Reverend Le Jau's good wife has looked to their care so far - with the help of some other good women. And they question now as to whether these girls are in fact Yamasee at all, as their dress and speech are very much unlike other Indians. Perhaps they were servants of some planter hereabouts - one no longer amongst the living."

"Ye've seen them then, sir?"

"Yes - Briefly - six of them. I did not hear them speak."

Pauline's eyes come alive again and David looks at her and smiles. He says, "Where is this parsonage, sir?"

"A short walk . We may catch the Reverend at church - and attend to both your matters there, eh - no time like the present?"

They leave the house and walk down the street.

CHAPTER 51

PAULINE MEETS REVEREND LE JAU

The Governor, Pauline and David walk to church - it's early afternoon and they find the Reverend in the chancel.

The Reverend notes their approach and says, "Good day to you, sir."

"Good day to you Reverend. I have a wedding proposition for you, sir."

"No - my daughters are still too young."

"No - not for myself - but for this pair here with me." The Governor turns to David and Pauline.

The Reverend looks and frowns. "I know them not. Have the Banns been posted in their parish? I'm sure I've seen none here." He looks more shrewdly at them. "They're not of the Presbytery are they?"

"No and no, sir."

"Any other sort of dissenters? Not Quakers I hope - God forbid."

"Definitely not Quakers." Here David grins a little.

"If they wish to be married in the Church I shall have to interview them first, of course. Now if it is convenient - and then we can post the first Bann at the evening service tonight."

The Governor takes a deep breath, then starts up.

"Look here Reverend Le Jau, this is Mister David Kilbernie, whom I'm sure you have heard of - and this is his affianced, Mistress Pauline Bray, of whom you may also have heard. They are the ones that sounded the Alarum cannon this Good Friday past." He cringes at the memory. "I have no doubt that without these young folk here we'd all be dead or caught up in a hard flight. They have saved this province once, sir, but their job is by no means finished. We need this pair to reestablish the peace with our former Siouxan allies to the north. Put plainly, we cannot fight the Yamassee - and the Creeks to the south, unless our north is secured. We must have peace with the Catawba to survive the winter here - and these two our best hope for that."

"Pauline is the subaltern of Reverend Raymond Bray, and a teacher in his ministry to the Indian Lands. She speaks the Siouxan tongue, and is a woman of renown amongst the tribes." He looks to her companion and nods at him.

"David is not a church member, but he has been in the wilderness entirely for the last three years - in the Indian Lands or traveling on militia business. He has been completely beyond communication, temptation, or opportunity these past three years to enter into any marriage contract. Say, when was the last time you even saw a white woman, David?"

"Until today? Well - three years now, I reckon. I landed in Port Royal September, 1712, and I hain't been in a town since then - not til today."

"So you see Reverend," the Governor says, "there is no one who could possibly offer cause to prevent this union. Let common sense prevail here sir. This is not England. And we owe a debt to these two here, make no mistake. -- For the good of the province, it is imperative that they leave here soon, and they want to marry before they depart. Exigent circumstances sometimes require especial expedience, no? Has the Bishop not already granted you extraordinary discretion in these lands? You who lead the largest parish in the Carolinas? -- No one would gainsay you on this matter. And it may well prove an ornament to your good name, sir, a testament to wisdom and blessed in remembrance - if in fact we do survive the next year here in these wild lands."

The Reverend closes his eyes - has a doubtful scowl and wonders if the young upstart of a 'Governor' is through - snortles a bit and says.

"Since she is, as you say, a relation to our esteemed Reverend Bray." He looks at Pauline.

"And as our crises here are most grievous... " Le Jau breathes in deep and closes his eyes. "I propose this. We call the Banns two times tonight at the evening service, before and after, and once again in the morning. If no one shows cause to prevent this union at that time." Le Jau looks at Pauline, and over to David. "They can be married then, on the morrow. "

David says, "Works for me." They turn and leave.

CHAPTER 52

A VERY HAPPY REUNION

When the girls see Pauline they squeal and come running out, grabbing her and making a babble. Rachel laments "They took the books - took them all - we lost everything mother."

Pauline hugs her and says "Fret not dear - we shall soon have more." Then hugs the little ones each in turn and murmurs something all through the happy reunion. She stands up straight and says.

"Praise be to God - I heard you all had the pox."

Sarah: (Speaking Creek) It was 3 -leaf, but...

Pauline says, "Speak in English here dear one, only English."

Sarah nods and continues, "But ... but the ladies here were so much - kinder - not like the... we did not dissuade them in their assumptions - nor their ministrations." Then she starts crying again.

The matron and her housekeeper are shocked. She says, "So you *have* taught them English - but have they been taught from the Prayer Book?"

Pauline says, "Oh yes, indeed. And I have read to them from King James's Bible also. Sarah and Rachel are learning the Catechism now, and ready for baptism, I believe. Would you care to hear?"

Matron Le Jau says, "Yes I would. Yes, indeed."

"I only have a copy of the 1548 - before revision. The Society could not spare a more recent edition."

"That's the one I have, from my great grandmother Mary - her own copy. Pray continue then. Let us hear the fruit of your instruction."

Pauline smiles at the matron's last words, then says, "Sarah - Rachel - Come and join hands with me. And you little deers come close too so that you may bear witness and learn."

Sarah and Rachel come up and take Pauline's hands - then extend their hands to the other four girls - who now form an ellipse on Pauline. She then looks to Sarah and asks,

"What is your Name?" And the young woman says, "Sarah"

Pauline then looks to Rachel and asks. "What is your Name?"

"Rachel"

Pauline then follows the role of the catechist, or instructor, as these two young and appealing women - with their Muscogee accents and clear complexions recite the refrains that have been recited by millions, the words of Thomas Cranmer relived again, on a pair of sweet soprano registers that harmonize together like they are twinned.

The governor turns away and leaves - his face suffused and red with emotion. David moves quickly after him and catches him outside.

"Governor! -- A moment sir."

The governor slows and turns around.

"They're yours - hers I mean. -- Take them with you when you leave. The Assembly will redeem their bond, or I will myself." He looks both angry and sad. "Take them. Consult with Burroughs on the details - it's a fair long trip."

"I know it well, sir - made it twice now."

"That you have - I forget. And I've only traveled the upcountry once you know - an astounding place - all those pristine rivers - beautiful. Even then - with all the distractions - the war - I could not help but think it a paradise on earth."

"And then the season turned on you."

"Well put that sir, yes, and then the season turned. -- And it could have all been avoided too. If Wright had not hounded Nairne with his incessant lawsuits - keeping him here at Court - I'm sure he could have fore fended this... all of this... this... waste... this madness.

"I didn't know, sir - and I was living right there in the middle of it."

"I pray God forgive me for my inattention nonetheless. This land is wild - too wild for me. A Governor's apt to grow old quick here, I think. -- Have you platted your claim?"

"No, I plan to today. I know a good site for a watermill - right on the fall line - ye should come and see it someday."

"Not likely, but thank you sir." He starts to turn and leave again.

"Oh and Governor - If I could importune here - just one more thing... "

CHAPTER 53

THE WEDDING

The mockingbird is on the ground this time hopping around - watching as the two youngest girls throw petals all around - tossing them up to a light grey morning sky, in the church garden, with harp music playing. The petals cover the ground around the girls - many colors. They have baskets in hand and plain cotton dresses. They walk a step - then toss petals. Pauline wears a finely stitched dress but no veil.

The Reverend calls out, "Who is here to give this woman in marriage?"

" I am." Answers the Governor.

CHAPTER 54

THE RETURN OF THE PRINCE

Pauline and David are leaving Charleston. The wedding dress is packed away now, and they're headed to the docks with the girls in tow, all with light carry baggage. Pauline sees a man across the street and stops.

"David, wait here a moment. That is our Inacua I see there. Let me have a word with him." She looks to the girls and says "Stay with David", in Creek and loud enough that the Prince hears and looks over.

The Prince is now homeless and destitute - a new beggar to the streets of Charleston in very fine, but worn English clothing - Creek in countenance but taller than most - English in manner.

Pauline walks across the street and he cries "Paulina" and starts to her. She holds her hands up, says in Creek "Stop!" Then in English "Sirician, what are you doing here? How are you here?"

"Living on these filthy streets, as you see - all alone. -- But I met the King - did you know? And when I came back I saw my people sold at the block - even bid on some with money from my patron, Mr. Johnson. But I purchased none - saved none. Johnson said prices were higher than usual, as there had been no Indian auctions in over two years now - 'They bid the girls up exceedingly high' he said. -- I hated him then - wanted him dead. And then the next day he was dead... drowned on a rowboat leaving to salvage some Spanish wreck. He just fell off the boat - right out in the harbor there (points). Just like that - in the space of days - every soul I know here either gone or dead. The room we letted on McAlvern Street was up - and since then I've... no means to .... I went to the fish gate and then to the hog gate thinking to slip away - but they are all closed now and guarded.

I can't escape this place. I'm so changed now from when you knew me. I have such thoughts - such terrible thoughts ." He is shaking all over. " And now - here you are. You! -- Why did you send me away Paulina? Why?

Pauline nods and grabs his right hand with both of hers. "You have learned much on your travels brother - and your English is much improved. I rejoice in seeing you alive and well." She takes a deep breath.

"And now... now that you are back - it is indeed fortuitous. I have yet another task for you brother - I pray thee - listen well -- (Deep breath) I am married now - to yon white man over there. You see him. He is called David Kilbernie and you should address him as Mister Kilbernie - and address me - address me now as Ma'am Kilbernie."

"So! -- We... David and I - we are preparing to leave this wretched town today - with a pair of scoutboats and 19 armed men - and 8 young ones of our people - those you see with David there. They are the ones who escaped."

"Brother... you will come with us now. You have journeyed far, and I want to hear of it, all of your stories. But I have been pressed upon a journey of my own now. One of my own making, if not my own devising. You are God sent. You must come with us."

"What - just - leave - leave with you now?"

"Yes. I know this is hard - but - please understand. I am newlywed today. Give us, me and David - give us some space for now. And later... me and him", she nods again and says, "You understand me. We shall be making our own tent - and you are to keep the watch for us. You do understand me now, Sirician?"

"No. I mean... I understand your meaning but..."

"Follow us for a bit anyway. We are heading to the docks, all packed and ready to go. You have until then to decide."

The prince looks like he's been punched in the gut, but says, "What else should I do?"

"I should let you know we're headed to the Waccamaw first, and then upriver to see Raymond again.

"Hah! Well - lead on then ma'am."

Pauline walks back across the street to the girls and David.

"He is the Euhaw prince, David, the Inacua. And he is just returned from England, where he met the King! He can speak the Sioux dialects better than I can, much better, and he has been there, lived amongst the Waccamaw, the Chicora, all the black glass Sioux. He has nothing here David, and no hope. He should come with us. He must come with us!"

"Is he another one of your dear ones?"

Pauline stops and grabs his arm to turn him facing her.

"David! We are married now and you are my husband, til death do us part. Did ye not just hear it from my own lips man!?" She's mad but trying to keep from a meltdown - deep breaths.

"And a gentleman does not ask about... certain things... ever! Or he shows himself to be less than a gentleman, Mister Kilbernie. Are we clear on that?"

David is taken aback a second - but collects himself, smiles, "Why - Yes... Yes indeed ... very clear, ma'am Kilbernie." Then he loops his arm back in hers and they start again toward the docks.

THE CITTERNS PART IN THE STORY

The citterns in this story are the 8 string variety that was as common in society back in the 1700's as the guitar is now. It served as the rhythm carrier for most songs back then. Citterns were roughly the size of a mandola, with an approximate scale of 20". Some were larger - up to the size of a modern day parlor guitar. Musicians from the time of King James wrote some fairly complicated arrangements with the cittern often taking the leading melody, like the lute usually did, but for the most part they were plucked and strummed with big bird quills - keeping the rhythm and projecting the music.

There is an album to accompany this book called:

Cittern Banjo The Music from Red Town White Town

Find it on Spotify - iTunes - Youtube etc.

For The Movie Producers

The sophisticated reader might very well think that there's more dialogue in this story than in an Elmore Leonard book. That's true enough, because I've always imagined this tale as a film and started on a sequel.

Acknowledgements

There are many non-fiction books out now about the Yamasee and Tuscarora wars. In Red Carolinians (1940) by Chapman James Millings, I first learned of the Yamasee and the Cusabo. The Cusabo helped the earliest settlers in Charles Town survive the first years by giving them corn and peas and teaching them about it's cultivation. But it was the Yamasee that enabled the settlers to thrive by offering them protection from the Spanish and other Indian tribes - and by offering them deerskins in trade - in abundance. Buckskins were the chief export of the colony and the base of all its commerce - this is how the term buck was first used to mean money.

From another book, The Yamasee Indians (2018), arranged by Denise Bossy, I came to understand that the Yamasee were not just raiders and slavers that replaced the Westos, but the chief diplomats and peacemakers for the region. They were a small people compared to the Creeks or Cherokee, but were held in high esteem by both. Their relative wealth and powers of influence far exceeded their numbers. And it was the Yamasee who effectively ended the Indian slave trade too, with their revolt and later intransigence to making peace with the Carolina colony. The deerskin and slave trade dropped to almost nothing for a couple of years, and the entire region of conflict was depopulated dramatically during the course of the wars.

The Yamasee never did make peace, though they were diminished and forced to move further and further south to avoid reprisals. And they did not stop making their own raids to the north. The Yamasee were formed from the chaos of war and slaving - from their beginning they were a polyglot mix of tribes and clans, and as they diminished they became the core of what would later be known as the Seminoles - another polyglot nation

- and those folks never did quite completely submit; not to the English, nor to the United States.